C000262480

THE CASE NOTES OF SHERLOCK HOLMES

THIS IS A CARLTON BOOK

Published in 2018 by Carlton Books Limited
20 Mortimer Street
London W1T 3JW

10 9 8 7 6 5 4 3 2 1

Text and artworks pp.8–149 © Metrostar Media Limited 2009
The rights of Guy Adams and Lee Thompson to be identified as the authors of this work have been asserted by them in accordance with the Copyright, Designs and Patents Act 1988.
Text and artworks pp.150–222 © Carlton Books 2015
Design © Carlton Books 2018

The text and images of this book previously appeared in *The Case Notes of Sherlock Holmes*, ISBN 978-0-233-00289-7 and *The Return of Sherlock Holmes: The Case Notes*, ISBN 978-0-233-00474-7

All rights reserved. This book is sold subject to the condition that it may not be reproduced, stored in a retrieval system or transmitted in any form or by any means, electronic, mechanical, photocopying, recording or otherwise without the publisher's prior consent.

A CIP catalogue record for this book is available from the British Library.

ISBN 978-1-78739-150-5

Printed in Dubai

THE CASE NOTES OF SHERLOCK HOLMES

DR JOHN WATSON &
SIR ARTHUR CONAN DOYLE

ANDRE
DEUTSCH

CONTENTS

INTRODUCTION 6

SHERLOCK HOLMES 8

A SCANDAL IN BOHEMIA 14

THE RED-HEADED LEAGUE 30

THE BOSCOMBE VALLEY MYSTERY 38

THE DANCING MEN 60

THE HOUND OF THE BASKERVILLES 78

THE FINAL PROBLEM 138

ADVENTURE OF THE EMPTY HOUSE 150

THE ADVENTURE OF THE NORWOOD BUILDER 168

THE ADVENTURE OF THE PRIORY SCHOOL 182

THE ADVENTURE OF THE SOLITARY CYCLIST 196

THE ADVENTURE OF BLACK PETER 210

CREDITS 224

AN INTRODUCTION

America has appeared frequently in the cases of Sherlock Holmes. In fact, the plains of Utah feature just as prominently in the narrative of Holmes' first ever recounted case, A Study in Scarlet, as the iconic streets of Britain's capital. Why then should I be in the least surprised that a trip to the U.S.A. would result in the most important Sherlockian discovery of all time?

I was working as an actor in those days and was about to embark on a tour of both the UK and America in a revival of *The Secret of Sherlock Holmes*, a play originally commissioned by actor Jeremy Brett to mark the centenary of Holmes' first publication. Preparation for the part — I can't begin to describe how seriously I took this venture — saw me in Florida during the summer of '06.

Florida is a strange place, a sunny fabrication, part fantasy-land part swamp. I love the area and have visited many times, though this trip was to be slightly different. It was in a steak restaurant just off I-4 that I met a retired gentleman whose contact details had been given to me by the producer of the revived show. The elderly gentleman's name will be familiar to many; Rafe McGregor was a retired literary professor from Edinburgh who claimed familial links with Doctor John Watson and had often been quoted as having inherited a number of the late doctor's literary effects. Despite frequent promises of allowing other scholars access to his papers he would inevitably beg some reason or other as to why he was unwilling to share. Truth be told he was something of a laughing stock, viewed by most as an attention-seeking sort.

Whatever the gentleman's reputation, I discovered he had retired close to my rented accommodation and it seemed foolishness not to meet up with the fellow. He was, somewhat to my surprise, amenable enough to the idea. Unfortunately, that enthusiasm didn't extend to the evening in question: he arrived at the restaurant more than half an hour late and was distinctly uncommunicative throughout the meal. He made allusions to "some old scrapbooks" but dismissed my best attempts to secure any examination of them. They would be of no interest, he insisted, and began to drink an amount rather more than I could comfortably match. Despite my natural inclination to disbelieve his claims — as so many others had — I admit I was intrigued by the man. I was convinced, despite all his alcoholic bluster, that there was

some truth to his claims. At no point, though, could I begin to crack through his refusal to let me see the documents alluded to and, while I saw a good deal of him during that visit, he gave no sign of relenting in his decision.

Years later, taking receipt of a large Jiffy bag from my postman, my brief association with McGregor was to come flooding back. It had appeared the old man's liver had finally given up the fight and a rather convivial attorney from Orlando was processing what little there was of his estate. Several chests of papers had been left to me but the man was unsure as to whether it was worth taking up my literary inheritance ("it smells of age rather than money" he explained in his note) but had enclosed a sample so I could decide. I had in my hands an old scrapbook, its pages loose and dry. As I began to read, I found myself almost terrified to turn those pages in case my enthusiasm might result in damaging them. During his accounts of the career of Sherlock Holmes, John Watson often referenced clippings and letters that he had preserved in scrapbooks over the years, an aide memoire for the time when he came to document the cases fully within the pages of *The Strand* magazine. The pages reeked of age, the ghosts of Persian tobacco and hair pomade, the flavours of no less inspiring a location than 221b Baker Street.

It is that first scrapbook that you find reproduced here, page for page. Unlike that most reticent of scholars, Rafe McGregor, I find my inclination is to share as widely as possible and it has been an act of great pleasure to allow the document to be photographed and reproduced as faithfully as possible within these pages. There has been some "tinkering", of course, but we have restricted ourselves as far as possible to the odd digital fix to clarify damaged areas of text, nips and tucks rather than wholesale revisions. Other than these tiny efforts to restore clarity what you find here is Watson's scrapbook, warts and all. I only hope it might inspire those new to the study of Sherlock Holmes to delve further into the life of this most amazing man and that of his chronicler and friend, Doctor John Watson.

Guy Adams

SHERLOCK HOLMES

Sherlock Holmes *seemed delighted at the idea of sharing his rooms with me. "I have my eye on a suite in Baker Street," he said, "which would suit us down to the ground. You don't mind the smell of strong tobacco, I hope?"*

"I always smoke 'ship's' myself," I answered.

"That's good enough. I generally have chemicals about, and occasionally do experiments. Would that annoy you?"

"By no means."

"Let me see – what are my other shortcomings? I get in the dumps at times, and don't open my mouth for days on end. You must not think I am sulky when I do that. Just let me alone, and I'll soon be right. What have you to confess now? It's just as well for two fellows to know the worst of one another before they begin to live together."

I laughed at this cross-examination. "I keep a bull pup," I said, "and I object to rows because my nerves are shaken, and I get up at all sorts of ungodly hours, and I am extremely lazy. I have another set of vices when I'm well, but those are the principal ones at present."

"Do you include violin playing in your category of rows?" he asked, anxiously.

"It depends on the player," I answered. "A well-played violin is a treat for the gods – a badly played one –"

"Oh, that's all right," he cried, with a merry laugh. "I think we may consider the thing as settled – that is if the rooms are agreeable to you."

Our rooms in Baker Street.

Holmes on Modesty:
"I cannot agree with those who rank modesty among the virtues. To the logician all things should be seen exactly as they are, and to underestimate one's self is as much a departure from truth as to exaggerate one's own powers."

Holmes' thoughts on detective fiction:
"Now, in my opinion, Dupin was a very inferior fellow. That trick of his of breaking in on his friends' thoughts with an apropos remark after a quarter of an hour's silence is really very showy and superficial. He had some analytical genius, no doubt; but he was by no means such a phenomenon as Poe appeared to imagine."

"Lecoq was a miserable bungler, he had only one thing to recommend him, and that was his energy. That book made me positively ill. The question was how

↗ *Edgar Allan Poe, and one of the illustrations from a tale of his where the monkey was the murderer! A small sketch of M. Lecoq, and one of the few sketches of Holmes looking calm and relaxed at a violin concerto.*

↑ *Holmes also has a profound knowledge of chemistry.*

to identify an unknown prisoner. I could have done it in twenty-four hours. Lecoq took six months or so. It might be made a textbook for detectives to teach them what to avoid."

My observations on Holmes' cocaine usage:

Holmes took his bottle from the corner of the mantel- piece and his hypodermic syringe from its neat morocco case. With his long, white, nervous fingers he adjusted the delicate needle, and rolled back his left shirt-cuff. For some little time his eyes rested thoughtfully upon the sinewy forearm and wrist all dotted and scarred with innumerable puncture-marks. Finally he thrust the sharp point home, pressed down the tiny piston, and sank back into the velvet-lined arm-chair with a long sigh of satisfaction.

And on his food habits:

It was one of his peculiarities that in his more intense moments he would permit himself no food, and I have known him to presume upon his iron strength until he has fainted from pure inanition.

A SCANDAL IN BOHEMIA

TUESDAY, 20 MARCH TO THURSDAY, 22 MARCH 1888

To Sherlock Holmes she is always The Woman.

I have seldom heard him mention her under any other name. In his eyes she eclipses and predominates the whole of her sex. It was not that he felt any emotion akin to love for Irene Adler. All emotions, and that one particularly, were abhorrent to his cold, precise but admirably balanced mind. He was the most perfect reasoning and observing machine that the world has seen, but as a lover he would have placed himself in a false position. He never spoke of the softer passions, save with a gibe and a sneer. They were admirable things for the observer – excellent for drawing the veil from men's motives and actions. But for the trained reasoner to admit such intrusions into his own delicate and finely adjusted temperament was to introduce a distracting factor which might throw a doubt upon all his mental results. Grit in a sensitive instrument would not be more disturbing than a strong emotion in a nature such as his. And yet there was but one woman to him, and that woman was Irene Adler…

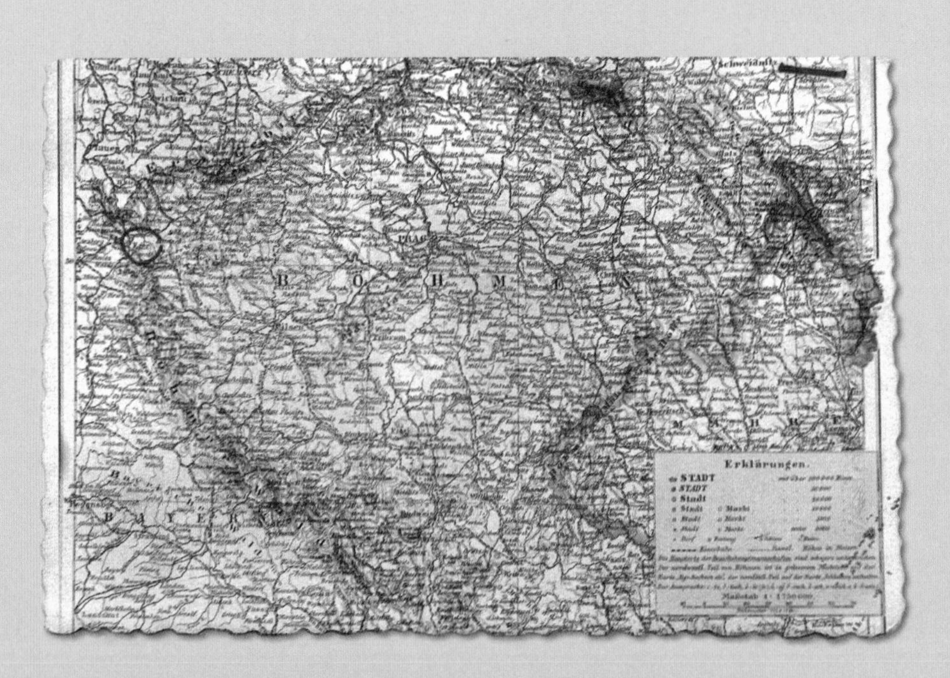

↑ *Egria – to the east of Bohemia.*

Dear Sherlock Holmes,

There will call upon you tonight, at a quarter to eight o'clock, a gentleman who desires to consult you upon a matter of the very deepest moment.

Your recent services to one of the royal houses of Europe have shown that you are one who may safely be trusted with matters which are of an importance which can hardly be exaggerated. This account of you we have from all quarters received.

Be in your chamber then at that hour, and do not take it amiss if your visitor wear a mask.

↓ *Our mysterious client.*

↑ *The letter was printed on strong, stiff paper which led me to assume the writer must surely be of means, a packet of such stock would cost at least half a crown in any London stationer. Holmes – as was so often the case – brought me up on my lazy assumption. The real interest, he insisted, lay in the peculiarity of the paper rather than its cost. Holding it up he discerned a barely visible papermark: EgP.Gt. His encyclopaedic mind for such things took no time in pinning it down as Egria Papier Gesellschaft – the mark of The Egria Paper Company, Egria being a small area of Bohemia. He further drew my attention to the language used within the note: 'This account of you we have from all quarters received' – "It is only the German," Holmes joked, "who is so uncourteous to his verbs."*

Our client was none other than the King of Bohemia, Wilhelm Gottsreich Sigismond von Ormstein. He had come from Prague, travelling incognito, solely to secure Holmes' services.

Five years ago, in Warsaw, his majesty had made the acquaintance of the adventuress, Irene Adler.

Holmes immediately surmised – correctly it would transpire – that his Majesty had committed the indiscretion of sending Adler compromising letters and now, on the eve of his marriage to Clotilde Lothman von Saxe-Meningen, second daughter of the King of Scandinavia, was desirous of getting them back.

Holmes was quick to point out that the onus of proof would lie with Adler, his Majesty's handwriting, notepaper or seal could all have been forged, stolen or imitated.

But there was the matter of a photograph it would seem, an image featuring the pair together. This was not to be so easily dismissed.

Ormstein, Wilhelm Gottsreich Sigismond von

Grand Duke of Cassel-Felstein, hereditary King of Bohemia.
Due shortly to be married to Clotilde Lothman von Saxe-Meningen (second daughter of the King of Scandinavia – whose strictness of morals should keep Wilhelm's nerves as taut as a viol string – he is a handsome young partygoer by all accounts and no stranger to romance).

Adler, Irene

Born in New Jersey in the year 1858.
Contralto. La Scala,
Prima donna Imperial Opera of Warsaw.
Retired from operatic stage now living in London.

↑ *He tore the mask from his face.*

Could the photograph not be bought? Holmes inquired. The lady refused to sell.

Stolen then? There had been five attempts already, his Majesty explained. Twice burglars in his employ had ransacked her house, twice the lady had been waylaid and once her luggage diverted. On none of the occasions had the slightest sign of the photograph been found.

But what was Adler's plan for the photograph? Nothing less than the complete ruination of his Majesty's reputation:

'She threatens to send the House of Scandinavia the photograph.' the King explained, 'And she will do it. I know that she will do it. You do not know her, but she has a soul of steel. She has the face of the most beautiful of women, and the mind of the most resolute of men. Rather than I should marry another woman, there are no lengths to which she would not go – none.'

Her plan, he concluded, was to send the photo on the very day that his forthcoming betrothal was publicly proclaimed: the following Monday.

↓ *Holmes' notes on the Adler residence:*

Briony Lodge, Serpentine Avenue, St John's Wood.
A bijou villa, built out up to the road but with a garden to the rear.
Large sitting room to the right,
well furnished, long front windows (easily opened).
Chubb lock on front door.

Holmes set out incognito to observe Irene Adler, what follows is a transcription of the report he gave me on his return:

There was a mews by the side of the house. I lent the ostlers a hand in rubbing down their horses, receiving twopence, a glass of half and half, two fills of shag tobacco, and as much information as I could desire about Miss Adler in exchange. She is the daintiest thing under a bonnet say the Serpentine-mews. Lives quietly, sings at concerts, drives out at five every day, returning at seven for dinner. Has only one male visitor who never calls less than once a day, and often twice. Mr. Godfrey Norton, a lawyer. That sounded ominous! Was she his client, his friend, or his mistress? If the former, she had probably transferred the photograph to his keeping. If the latter, it was less likely.

While there I saw a hansom cab drive up and a gentleman – who I took to be Norton – spring out. He appeared to be in a great hurry. He was in the house about half an hour, and I caught glimpses

Mr. Godfrey Norton – a lawyer.
his client, his friend, or his mistress?

'Drive like the devil,' he shouted,
to the Church of St. Monica in
the Edgeware Road.

Jumped into the next cab

All three stood in front of the altar.
Norton: Only three minutes, or it
won't be legal.'

Assisting in the tying up of Irene Adler
to Godfrey Norton.

The bride gave me a sovereign

of him in the sitting-room windows talking excitedly. Presently he emerged and stepped up to the cab. "Drive like the devil," he shouted, "first to Gross & Hankey's in Regent Street, and then to the Church of St Monica in the Edgware Road. Half a guinea if you do it in twenty minutes!" Away they went. Next came Adler's own landau, hastily prepared.

Holmes in Disguise – Holmes in the character of a groom out of work, ill-kempt and side-whiskered, with an inflamed face and disreputable clothes. Accustomed as I was to my friend's amazing skill in disguises, I had to look three times before I was certain that it was he. ↓

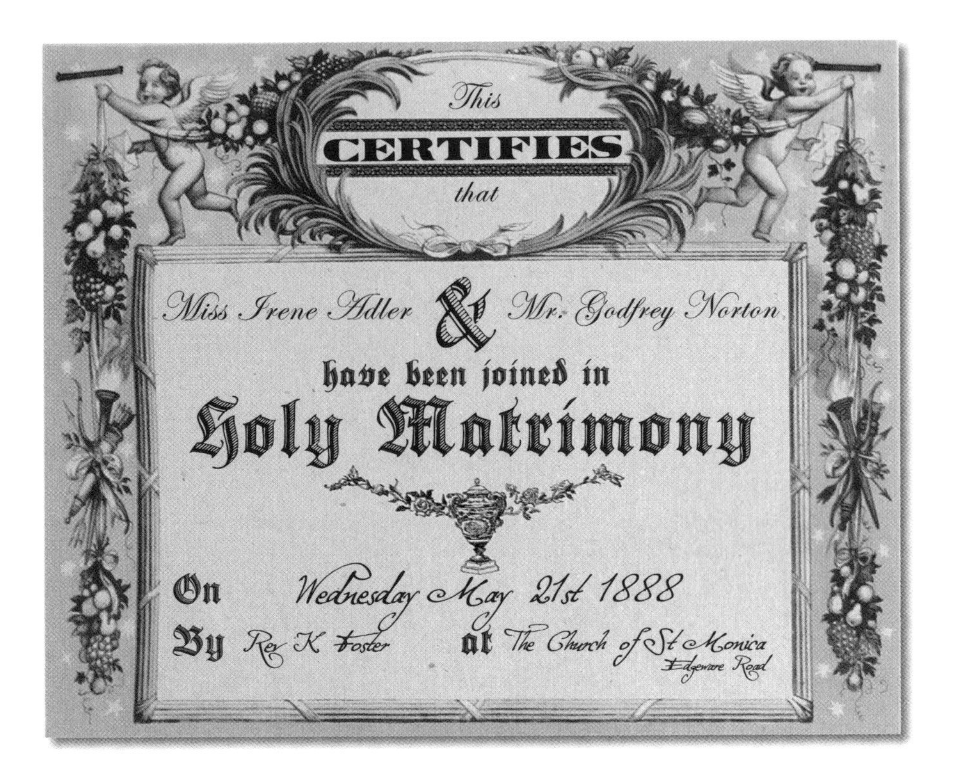
This CERTIFIES that
Miss Irene Adler & Mr. Godfrey Norton
have been joined in
Holy Matrimony
On Wednesday May 21st 1888
By Rev K Foster at The Church of St Monica
Edgeware Road

She shot out of the hall door and into it. "The Church of St Monica, John," she cried, "and half a sovereign if you reach it in twenty minutes."This was quite too good to lose! I jumped into the next cab to pass by and repeated the offer of half a sovereign to the driver for his speedy arrival at The Church of St Monica.

The cab and the landau were in front of the church door when I arrived. I paid the man and hurried inside. There was not a soul there save the two whom I had followed and a surpliced clergyman. All three stood in a knot in front of the altar. Suddenly, to my surprise, they turned in my direction. Godfrey Norton came running towards me.

"Thank God," he cried. "You'll do. Only three minutes, or it won't be legal."

I was dragged up to the altar, and found myself generally assisting in the tying up of Irene Adler to Godfrey Norton. It was done in an instant. The bride gave me a sovereign, and I mean to wear it on my watch-chain in memory of the occasion.

But, I found my plans seriously menaced! It looked as if the pair might take an immediate departure, necessitating prompt and energetic measures on my part. At the church door, however, they separated, he driving back to the Temple, and she to her own house. 'I shall drive out in the park at five as usual,' she said as she left him. They drove away in different directions, and I went off to make my own arrangements.

Holmes warned me that: "There will probably be some unpleasantness." This was hardly unusual!

I was again struck by the innate dramatist in my friend. He would never construct fictions for the sake of it – to him such an act was trivial and bizarre – and yet when a case called for elaborate plotting and performance he leapt to the challenge with aplomb. I suppose it was his consummate understanding of human nature, it allowed him to "become" the false characters he constructed from wax, wigs and makeup and also to devise elaborate chunks of theatre that would see his selected audience respond in the manner he wished. If one understood everything about human nature, manipulating it was no great task.

Holmes explained the bare-bones of his plan: he would be conveyed into the house of Irene Adler (at the time I knew better than to ask how) thereafter I was to wait four or five minutes until the large sitting-room window was opened. At that point Holmes would signal to me and I was to hurl the plumber's smoke rocket he had provided through the open window and raise the alarm of "fire!". My part thus played I would retire to the corner of the street where he would join me once free to do so.

→ *Holmes within a new disguise.*

London Standard

ST. JOHN'S WOOD FRACAS

It is a sad fact of modern living that violence is no longer restricted to the slum. Barbarity has always been the currency of the impoverished and the immigrant and when spent only within the environment of society's dregs it was something to which right-thinking citizens could 'turn a blind eye'. Now, however, nowhere is safe and we are forced to be ever alert.

Last night, an example of this common savagery was witnessed in St. John's Wood, adjacent to the home of respected contralto Miss. Irene Adler. The point of instigation remains unclear, although a number of reports suggest a disagreement between a pair of guardsmen and a street-trader may well have been the spark to the tinder. Brawling will always draw a crowd amongst those starved of the healthier entertainments and a sizable gathering had formed by the time Miss Adler returned from a drive in the park. Spotting an opportunity for quick gain, a pair of ruffians made to snatch at the lady's purse and would have succeeded were it not for the timely intervention of a passing clergyman who fought his way to Miss Adler's side, fearing for her safety. The elderly gentlemen was no match for the might of the crowd and was struck a blow to the head. The clergyman fell to the ground and the crowd dissipated, their cowardly streak now revealed through fear of the law. Miss Adler, recognising the elderly gentleman's heroism, conducted his unconscious body – not, thankfully, dead as the crowd had no doubt feared –° into her home so that his wound could be dressed.

Sadly that was not an end to the night's tribulations as scant minutes later smoke was seen erupting from her home and a general alarm of fire was raised. As the smoke began to clear its source was recognised as a rocket used by plumbers for testing the integrity of pipes and it is assumed that the article was thrown by the departing gang by way of retribution. It is some small consolation that nobody appears to have been hurt. The clergyman was seen leaving Miss Adler's house shortly after but we have been unable to trace him for further comment.

← *A report of the fray in the* London Standard.

↓ *He gave a cry as he fell…*

THE NEWLY REFURBISHED EMPIRE THEATRE OF VARIETIES LEICESTER SQR.

PRESENTS THE AMAZING OPERATIC STYLINGS OF

IRENE ADLER

FRIDAY APRIL 22

SATURDAY APRIL 23

FOR TWO PERFORMANCES ONLY!

An Evening of Wonderful Entertainment for Ladies and Gentlemen
also presenting the following artistes for your enjoyment

THE ALL-NEW LONDON BALLET TROUPE REVUE

To celebrate the new season of performances at the new Empire Theatre of the Varieties, with delightful sets from the craftsmanship of C. Wilhelm, we proudly introduce the spectacular London Ballet Troupe, performing scenes from the ballet shows from all across the globe. Marvel at their poise, their grace, their equisite costumes, their remarkable talent, but – above all – become enchanted with their beauty!

THE MINIATURE MALTESE PIANIST

Under the teachings of R Shearmann, this amazing feat of nature and music combines to show a rousing rendition of some of the world's most complex piano symphonies. A pigmy man from the depths of the British Empire, on the boat passage to India, was discovered with a remarkable talent on the ivories – he truly needs to be seen to be believed!

MADAME BRODY AND HER SINGING DOG

A brand-new variety act sure to amuse and amaze! Madame Brody, plucked from a fine East-End public house with her amazing performing beagle hound, Napoleon, sing such classic tavern favourites as 'Knees up Mother Brown' and 'Roll Out The Barrel' – sure to get every patron singing and applauding with joy!

EMPIRE THEATRE OF VARIETIES, LEICESTER

← *A performance poster of one of the rare London appearances by Irene Adler, at the then-named Empire Theatre of Varieties in Leicester Square.*

→ *On our return my friend was greeted by what appeared to be a thin youth in an Ulster who was hurrying by.*

Holmes explained the intent of the night's piece of theatre afterwards, though I had begun to guess during those tense minutes while I waited outside. When a woman thinks her house is on fire, she rushes to the thing she values most. At the moment the cry of "fire" rang out, Irene Adler revealed the location of the photograph – in a recess just above the bell-pull – by moving towards it, intent on securing the item's safety.

Holmes was elated on the journey home, removing his disguise and chuckling over his methods. The only crack in his good humour appeared when, on our return to Baker Street, a passing stranger bade him a good evening. It seemed a perfectly innocent occurrence to me but there was clearly something about it that unsettled Holmes…

Clarification on that opening line: "In the company of our most illustrious client, we returned to St. John's Wood the next morning and paid a visit to the home of Miss Irene Adler. Of the house's mistress there was no sign. The housekeeper explained that she had left with Norton on the 5.15 from Charing Cross, bound for the continent never to return. The housekeeper passed a letter to Holmes:

My Dear Mr. Sherlock Holmes:

You really did it very well. You took me in completely. Until after the alarm of fire, I had not a suspicion. But then, when I found how I had betrayed myself, I began to think. I had been warned against you months ago. I had been told that if the King employed an agent it would certainly be you. And your address had been given me. Yet, with all this, you made me reveal what you wanted to know. Even after I became suspicious, I found it hard to think evil of such a dear, kind old clergyman. But, you know, I have been trained as an actress myself. Male costume is nothing new to me. I often take advantage of the freedom which it gives. I sent John, the coachman, to watch you, ran up stairs, got into my walking-clothes, as I call them, and came down just as you departed.

Well, I followed you to your door, and so made sure that I was really an object of interest to the celebrated Mr. Sherlock Holmes. Then I, rather impudently, wished you good-night, and started for the Temple to see my husband.

We both thought the best resource was flight, when pursued by so formidable an antagonist; so you will find the nest empty when you call to-morrow. As to the photograph, your client may rest in peace. I love and am loved by a better man than he. The King may do what he will without hindrance from one whom he has cruelly wronged. I keep it only to safeguard myself, and to preserve a weapon which will always secure me from any steps which he might take in the future. I leave a photograph which he might care to possess; and I remain, dear Mr. Sherlock Holmes,

Very truly yours,

Irene Norton, nee Adler

Holmes was keen to retain the photograph of Miss Adler.

"What a woman!" the King of Bohemia cried. "Would she not have made an admirable queen? Is it not a pity that she was not on my level?"

"From what I have seen" Holmes replied coldly, "she seems indeed to be on a very different level to your Majesty."

We feared that our client might be disappointed by what was terrible failure in Holmes' eyes.

"On the contrary," the King replied, "Her word is inviolate.

The photograph is now as safe as if it were in the fire."

So relieved was he by the outcome that he wished to offer Holmes an extra token of his appreciation. Not caring for gold or trinkets Holmes made his request: Irene's photograph. Though startled the King was happy to grant the request and my friend guards the image as a most precious object indeed: The Woman who beat Sherlock Holmes.

THE RED-HEADED LEAGUE

THURSDAY, 9 OCTOBER TO FRIDAY, 10 OCTOBER 1890

The details in the case of Mr Jabez Wilson:

He owned a small pawnbroker's business at Coburg Square, near the City and used to keep two assistants, but now only one: Vincent Spaulding (who accepted half wages so as to learn the business). Spaulding had an interest in photography and frequently used the cellar of Mr Wilson's business as a dark room. It was Spaulding who drew his employer's attention to the newspaper clipping concerning The Red-headed League.

Wilson – like I – had no knowledge of the league but Spaulding informed him of their alleged history: a company of two hundred persons, founded by American millionaire Ezekiah Hopkins who charged his trustees to make life comfortable for people with hair as red as his own.

Wilson, though sceptical, travelled to the office mentioned in the article and waited for an interview alongside a good number of similarly red-headed gentlemen. The office was bare but for a pair of chairs and a deal table. Wilson was interviewed by a man named Duncan Ross and found himself employed on the spot, offered the hours between 10 and 2 (which fitted most conveniently with his own business) at a wage of 4 pounds a week. The work was most strange, bound to his office within those hours – to leave was to forfeit his position – and copy out the Encyclopedia Britannica. He was to provide his own paper, ink and pens.

rning Chronicle

TO THE RED-HEADED LEAGUE:

On account of the bequest of the late Ezekiah Hopkins, of Lebanon, Pennsylvania, U. S. A., there is now another vacancy open which entitles a member of the League to a salary of 4 pounds a week for purely nominal services.

All red-headed men who are sound in body and mind and above the age of twenty-one years, are eligible.

Apply in person on Monday, at eleven o'clock, to Duncan Ross, at the offices of the League, 7 Pope's Court, Fleet Street.

↑ *The card found pinned to the door of 7 Pope's Court that drove Wilson to consult with Holmes.*

He arrived at the League's offices to find everything as described and set to the bizarre task of transcribing the Encyclopaedia provided. This strange task became his occupation for eight weeks, Ross receiving his written pages with enthusiasm as fast as he could provide them. Then, on the morning of October the 9th he viewed the above sign and resolved to seek assistance in solving the puzzle.

ANGUSSOLA or ANGUSSCIOLA, Italian portrait painter of the latter half of the 16th century, was born at Cremona about 1535, and died at Palermo in 1626. In 1560, at the invitation of Philip II., she visited the court of Madrid, where her portraits elicited great commendation. Vandyck is said to have declared that he had derived more knowledge of the true principles of his art from her conversation than from any other source. She painted several fine portraits of herself, one of which is at Althorp. A few specimens of her painting are to be seen at Florence and Madrid. She had three sisters, who were also celebrated artists.

ANHALT, a duchy of Germany, and a constituent state of the German empire, formed, in 1863, by the amalgamation of the two duchies Anhalt-Dessau-Cöthen and Anhalt-Bernburg. The country now known as Anhalt consists of two larger portions—Eastern and Western Anhalt, separated by the interposition of a part of Prussian Saxony—and of five enclaves surrounded by Prussian territory, viz. Alsleben, Mühlingen, Dornburg, Gödnitz and Tilkerode-Abberode. The eastern and larger portion of the duchy is enclosed by the Prussian government district of Potsdam

Pages carefully transcribed by Mr Wilson whilst under the employ of the League.

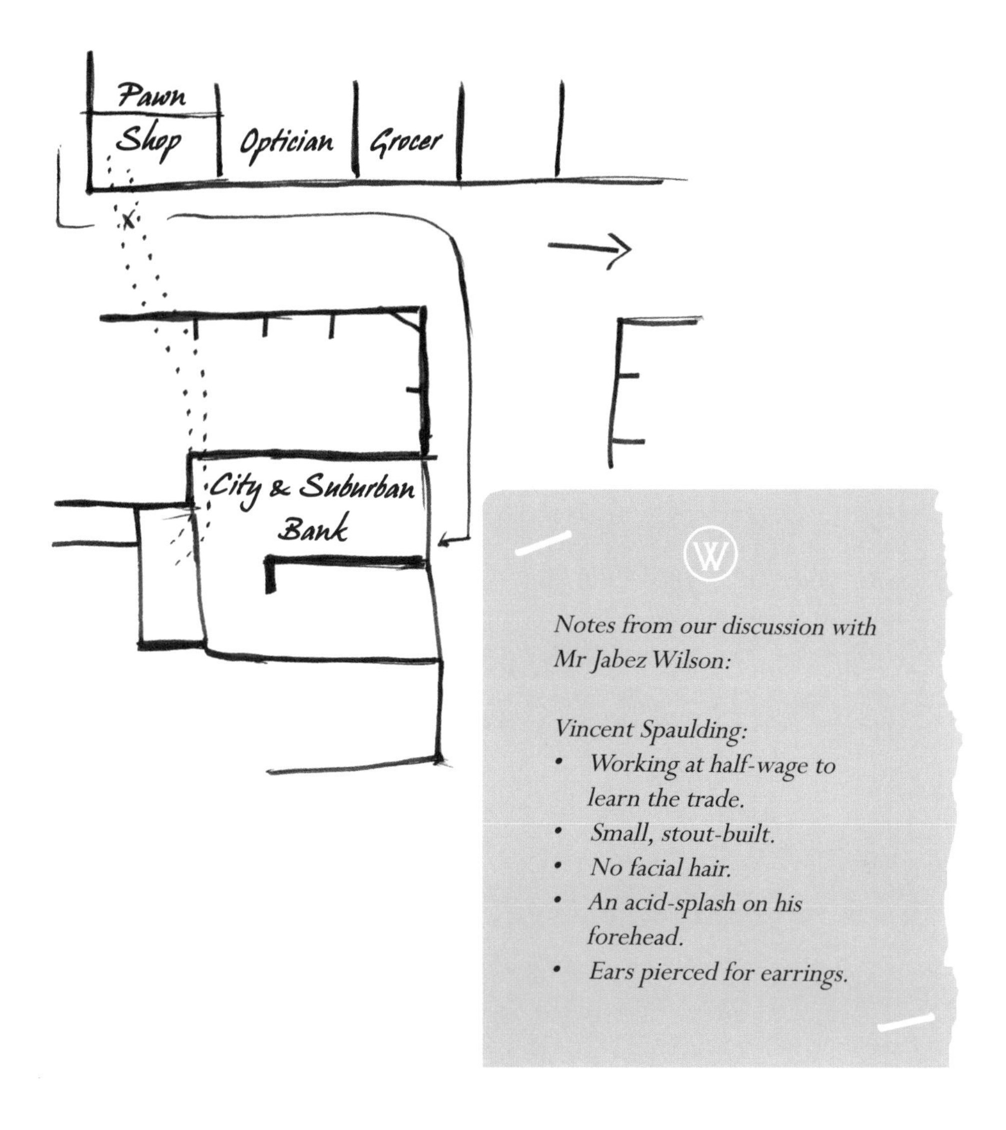

Holmes declared the matter a "three-pipe problem" and demanded I not disturb him while he cogitated.

An hour or so later he burst forth with great energy and invited me to a performance by Sarasate that afternoon. Having little at my practice to distract me I agreed.

We took a detour via Saxe-Coburg square and Mr. Wilson's pawnshop. Holmes behaved in a most unusual manner, tapping his cane heartily on the pavement before enquiring the way to The Strand from Wilson's assistant, Spaulding. I quite understood this to be a ruse in order to allow Holmes a glance at the man, and told him so. My friend laughed and commented that it had not been the man's face that he wished to see – Wilson's description had already identified the man to him as John Clay, a villain of some repute – but rather his knees.

But what interest were the man's knees? He would not be drawn, merely insisting that we should return under cover of darkness with the assistance of Scotland Yard.*

**It would later become clear of course that Holmes was hunting for signs that the man had been digging.*

BANK STOCKPILE RUMOUR IN CITY

It has been reported that the City & Suburban Bank has secured the loan of 30,000 gold Napoleons from The Bank of France in order to strengthen their resources.

When contacting the chairman of the directors, Mr. James Merryweather, for clarification he refused to discuss the subject though he did comment that such a reserve of bullion would be inordinately large for a single branch.

Clay, John
Grandfather was a royal duke.
Schooled at Eton and Oxford.
His brain is as cunning as his fingers, considerable experience in criminal entry but singularly elusive. Though I hear of his handiwork at almost every turn I have yet to set eyes on him.

<u>Distinguishing features</u>: White 'acid' stain of his forehead, pierced earlobes.

The Morning Chr

LONDON'S

INFAMOUS BANK ROBBER BROUGHT TO JUSTICE

Yesterday saw the famed criminal John Clay finally brought to justice. Clay, responsible for such notorious robberies as the Billingsley Deposit Job and the audacious Frennington Vault heist (much discussed in financial circles even now) had recently been employed within the pawnbroking business of a Mr Jabez Wilson in Saxe-Coburg Square. Unsurprisingly, the job was no more than a ruse. Working within that location offered Clay a means of subterranean access to the vault of the adjacent City & Suburban Bank (where, as we reported some weeks ago, it is believed a sizeable quantity of French gold was being stored). Over the past several weeks Clay had been digging a tunnel between the two buildings having otherwise detained his employer in a fictitious position as a member of 'The Red-Headed League'.

CLAY NOT WORKING ALONE
SHERLOCK HOLMES LIKELY DRAFTED IN TO ASSIST WITH INVESTIGATION

Clay and his accomplice, Archie Morris, were caught within the vault last night by representatives of Scotland Yard (under the able eye of Inspector Jones), the chairman of the directors of City & Suburban Bank, Mr James Merryweather and two other gentlemen whose identities were being withheld from the press but which this reporter might be so bold as to suggest could have been none other than famed sleuth Sherlock Holmes and his friend and chronicler Doctor John Watson. Certainly it is known that Mr Holmes has taken a considerable interest in the career of Clay (as far as being desirous of ending it) and Clay's reputation is such that it might be imagined such a legendary personage as Sherlock Holmes would be required to match it.

Two clippings from the Morning Chronicle *detailing the bank's horde of Napoleons (from 25 August 1890) and the capture of John Clay (from 30 October 1890) – with mention of Holmes' involvement.*

THE BOSCOMBE VALLEY MYSTERY

MONDAY, 3 JUNE TO THURSDAY, 27 JUNE 1889

A.
Prefix RPO45 Code UG657

POST OFFICE TELEGRAPHS.

No. of Message

For URGENT delivery to

Words	Sent
1	At LDN-OX
Charge	To LDN
1	By S MCKAY

(A Receipt for the Charges on this Telegram can be obtained, price one penny.)

FROM

Please Write Distinctly.

Sherlock Holmes

Addresses Free.

To: Doctor John Watson

1/- HAVE YOU A COUPLE OF DAYS TO SPARE? HAVE JUST BEEN WIRED FOR FROM THE WEST OF ENGLAND IN CONNECTION WITH BOSCOMBE VALLEY TRAGEDY.

1/3 SHALL BE GLAD IF YOU WILL COME WITH ME. AIR AND

1/6 SCENERY PERFECT. LEAVE PADDINGTON BY THE 11:15.

SENDER ~~OF THIS TELEGRAM.~~

Regulations made pursuant to the 15th Section of the Telegraph Act, 1868.

(HARRISON & SONS, PRINTERS, LONDON

1982 GREAT WESTERN RAILWAY
London, Paddington.
LDN. PADDINGTON
TO
ROSS
FIRST CLASS
1982

1658 GREAT WESTERN RAILWAY
London, Paddington.
LDN. PADDINGTON
TO
ROSS
FIRST CLASS – FARE 6d
Issued subject to the Company's Printed Conditions & Regulations
NOT TRANSFERABLE
1658

VALLEY DEATH

Body found by lake in Boscombe Valley

The residents of Boscombe Valley are shocked this morning to hear of the death of Mr Charles McCarthy whose body was found at the Boscombe Pool, a quarter of a mile from his home at Hatherly Farm. More details are sparse at present but it is believed that the man died from being struck repeatedly in the head. He leaves a son of eighteen, Mr. James McCarthy – currently believed to be in police custody – but no wife or other dependents.

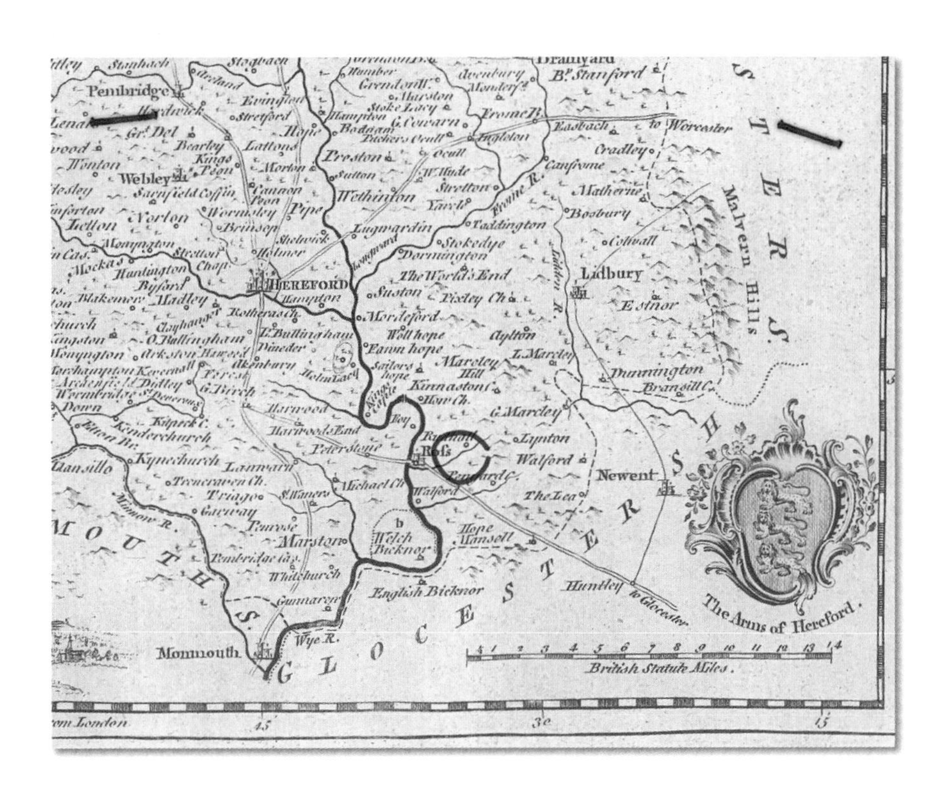

↑ *Boscombe Valley, just south of Ross*

← *Tuesday 4 June, 1889 – the first article in the* Herefordshire Times *on the death of McCarthy.*

Herefordshire Times

McCARTHY MURDER
BOSCOMBE VALLEY MYSTERY

Witnesses at Inquest Reveal Details

Deceased's Son Held For Questioning

More details have come to light in the violent death of Mr. Charles McCarthy as reported yesterday. Mr. McCarthy was an ex-patriot of Australia tenanted to Mr. John Turner (also a one-time resident in the Antipodes) who owns a good deal of land in the area. Despite the clear disparity in the estates of the gentlemen it is understood that both lived in perfect equality having known one another in the colonies before choosing to settle on our shores a number of years ago. They lived somewhat isolated lives from the local community though Mr. McCarthy and his eighteen-year-old son James (who has been arrested for the murder of his father) were regularly seen at local race-meetings.

On Monday morning Mr. McCarthy had been in Ross with his serving man and was overheard to note that he had a meeting of great importance at three o'clock and must return to the farm in order to keep it. At the given time he left the farm on foot and began walking the quarter mile to Boscombe Pool. He was seen on that journey by two witnesses, an elderly lady who had been gathering medicinal herbs and William Crowder, a gamekeeper to Mr. John Turner. Both witnesses confirm that Mr. McCarthy was quite alone though Mr. Crowder further reports that he saw Mr. James McCarthy following on some minutes later carrying a gun under his arm. Mr. Crowder explained at the police inquest today that he had no cause to mark the fact as suspicious at the time, it was only later when he heard of Mr. McCarthy's death that it seemed relevant. James McCarthy, having reported the discovery of his father's body at the Boscombe Valley lodge house, was immediately taken into custody.

A further witness was presented at the police inquest: Miss Patience Moran, the fourteen-year-old daughter of the lodge keeper. Miss Moran was picking flowers in the woods that border Boscombe Pool when she overheard the victim and his son in heated argument, She testified that Mr. McCarthy used extremely strong language towards his son who, clearly agitated, raised his hand to the old man by way of retaliation. Miss Moran, scared by the possibility of violence, ran away from the scene and returned home to her mother. It was only moments after that James McCarthy arrived at the lodge to ask for help. Mr. McCarthy was much excited and his right hand and sleeve were observed by Mrs. Moran to be stained by blood. It is noted also that he was without his gun at this juncture, it being later found by the body of his father. The injuries would be consistent with a beating from the blunt-end of the rifle and so it has been retained as a possible murder weapon.

While James McCarthy attests to his innocence the inquest has returned a verdict of "wilful murder" and the case will be presented before the magistrates at Ross later today.

Wednesday 5 June, 1889 – a rather inclusive article in the Herefordshire Times *on the "mystery", followed by the details of the case being referred to the next assizes court session (from the Thursday 6 June paper).*

McCARTHY MURDER
ENQUIRY CASE ESCALATED

Further to the case against Mr. James McCarthy in the murder of his father on Monday 3 June, the Ross Magistrates have referred the case to the next assizes.

← *They found the body.*

↓ *Friday, 7 June, 1888 – a further article from the* Herefordshire Times, *who seemed to relish this news story and reported it in much detail.*

Mr. James McCarthy, the only son of the deceased, was then called and gave evidence as follows:

"I had been away from home for three days at Bristol, and had only just returned upon the morning of last Monday, the 3rd. My father was absent from home at the time of my arrival, and I was informed by the maid that he had driven over to Ross with John Cobb, the groom.

"Shortly after my return I heard the wheels of his trap in the yard, and, looking out of my window, I saw him get out and walk rapidly out of the yard, though I was not aware in which direction he was going. I then took my gun and strolled out in the direction of the Boscombe Pool, with the intention of visiting the rabbit-warren which is upon the other side. On my way I saw William Crowder, the game-keeper, as he had stated in his evidence; but he is mistaken in thinking that I was following my father. I had no idea that he was in front of me. When about a hundred yards from the pool I heard a cry of 'Cooee!' which was a usual signal between my father and myself. I then hurried forward, and found him standing by the pool. He appeared to be much surprised at seeing me and asked me rather roughly what I was doing there. A conversation ensued which led to high words and almost to blows, for my father was a man of a very violent temper. Seeing that his passion was becoming ungovernable, I left him and returned towards Hatherley Farm. I had not gone more than 150 yards, however, when I heard a hideous outcry behind me, which caused me to run back again. I found my father expiring upon the ground, with his head terribly injured. I dropped my gun and held him in my arms, but he almost instantly expired. I knelt beside him for some minutes, and then made my way to Mr. Turner's lodge-keeper, his house being the nearest, to ask for assistance. I saw no one near my father when I returned, and I have no idea how he came by his injuries.

"He was not a popular man, being somewhat cold and forbidding in his manners, but he had, as far as I know, no active enemies. I know nothing further of the matter."

The Coroner: Did your father make any statement to you before he died?

Witness: He mumbled a few words, but I could only catch some allusion to a rat.

The Coroner: What did you understand by that?

Witness: It conveyed no meaning to me. I thought that he was delirious.

The Coroner: What was the point upon which you and your father had this final quarrel?

Witness: I should prefer not to answer.

The Coroner: I am afraid that I must press it.

Witness: It is really impossible for me to tell you. I can assure you that it has nothing to do with the sad tragedy which followed.

The Coroner: That is for the court to decide. I need not point out to you that your refusal to answer will prejudice your case considerably in any future proceedings which may arise.

Witness: I must still refuse.

The Coroner: I understand that the cry of "Cooee" was a common signal between you and your father?

Witness: It was.

The Coroner: How was it, then, that he uttered it before he saw you, and before he even knew that you had returned from Bristol?

Witness (with considerable confusion): I do not know.

A Juryman: Did you see nothing which aroused your suspicions when you returned on hearing the cry and found your father fatally injured?

Witness: Nothing definite.

The Coroner: What do you mean?

Witness: I was so disturbed and excited as I rushed out into the open, that I could think of nothing except of my father. Yet I have a vague impression that as I ran forward something lay upon the ground to the left of me. It seemed to me to be something grey in colour, a coat of some sort, or a plaid perhaps. When I rose from my father I looked round for it, but it was gone.

The Coroner: Do you mean that it disappeared before you went for help?

Witness: Yes, it was gone.

The Coroner: You cannot say what it was?

Witness: No, I had a feeling something was there.

The Coroner: How far from the body?

Witness: A dozen yards or so.

The Coroner: And how far from the edge of the wood?

Witness: About the same.

The Coroner: Then if it was removed it was while you were within a dozen yards of it?

Witness: Yes, but with my back towards it.

This concluded the examination of the witness.

↑ *James had him in his arms.*

On our arrival Holmes and I were met by the daughter of Mr John Turner who was quick to assure us that James McCarthy was innocent.

Miss Turner: James never did it. And about his quarrel with his father, I am sure that the reason why he would not speak about it to the coroner was because I was concerned in it.

It is no time for me to hide anything. James and his father had many disagreements about me. Mr McCarthy was very anxious that there should be a marriage between us. James and I have always loved each other as brother and sister; but of course he is young and has seen very little of life yet, and he naturally did not wish to do anything like that yet. So there were quarrels, and this, I am sure, was one of them."

Holmes: Was your father in favour of such a union?

Miss Turner: No, he was averse to it also. No one but Mr McCarthy was in favour of it.

When enquiring as to whether we might be allowed to visit Mr Turner it was explained that his health was poor. The death of Mr McCarthy had affected him badly as he had been the only man alive to know him from the gold mines in Victoria where he had made his considerable fortunes.

← *Alice Turner visited us.*

Ross Coroners Offices
SURGEON MEDICAL REPORT

Surgeon: Doctor S Aber *Subject:* Charles McCarthy *Date:* June ☐th

The posterior third of the left parietal bone and the left half of the occipital bone have been shattered by a heavy blow from a blunt weapon.

The likelihood therefore is that the assailant approached the victim from behind. While we cannot confirm the gun as the murder weapon — it certainly bears no traces of having been used in such action — nor can we deny its efficacy for the task.

Doctor S. Al

THE ROYAL OAK
PUBLIC HOUSE
OLD S^t, LIVERPOOL

James,

I has seen your face in the papers and even here tongues wag as to the terrible thing what you 've done.

It is a great relief to me that our marriage was not legal for I already has an husband.

He is from the Bermuda Dockyard and rest ashured that if you ever gets out he will waste no time in hunting you down shoulds you try to come anywhere near me.

Doreen.

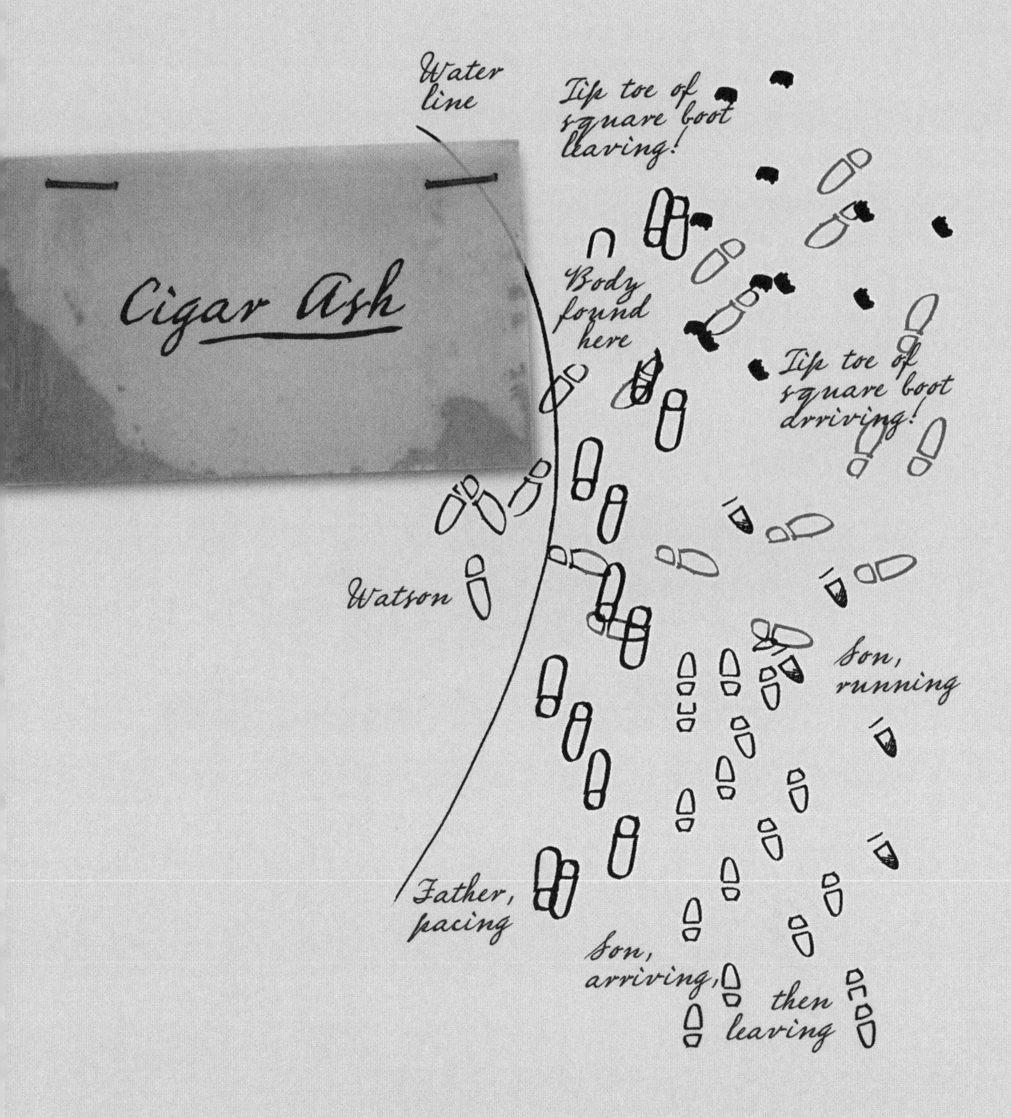

Lestrade joined us for breakfast (he was utterly convinced of young James McCarthy's guilt, but the day Holmes bases his thoughts on Lestrade's convictions will be the day he retires!).

He informed us that John Turner's health was so degenerated that the man's life was despaired of. He was about sixty and the general consensus on the subject of his health was that his constitution had been shattered by life abroad.

Holmes was startled by the news that Turner had always allowed the McCarthys to stay at Hatherly Farm rent free.

Holmes: Does it not strike you as singular that this McCarthy, who appears to have had little of his own, and to have been under such obligations to Turner, should still talk of marrying his son to

Turner's daughter, who is, presumably, heiress to the estate, and that in such a very cocksure manner, as if it were merely a case of a proposal and all else would follow? It is the more strange, since we know that Turner himself was averse to the idea. The daughter told us as much. Do you not deduce something from that?

Observations on the killer drawn from Holmes' investigation of the scene of crime:

He is a tall man, left-handed, limps with the right leg, wears thick-soled shooting-boots and a grey cloak, smokes Indian cigars, uses a cigar-holder, and carries a blunt pen-knife in his pocket.

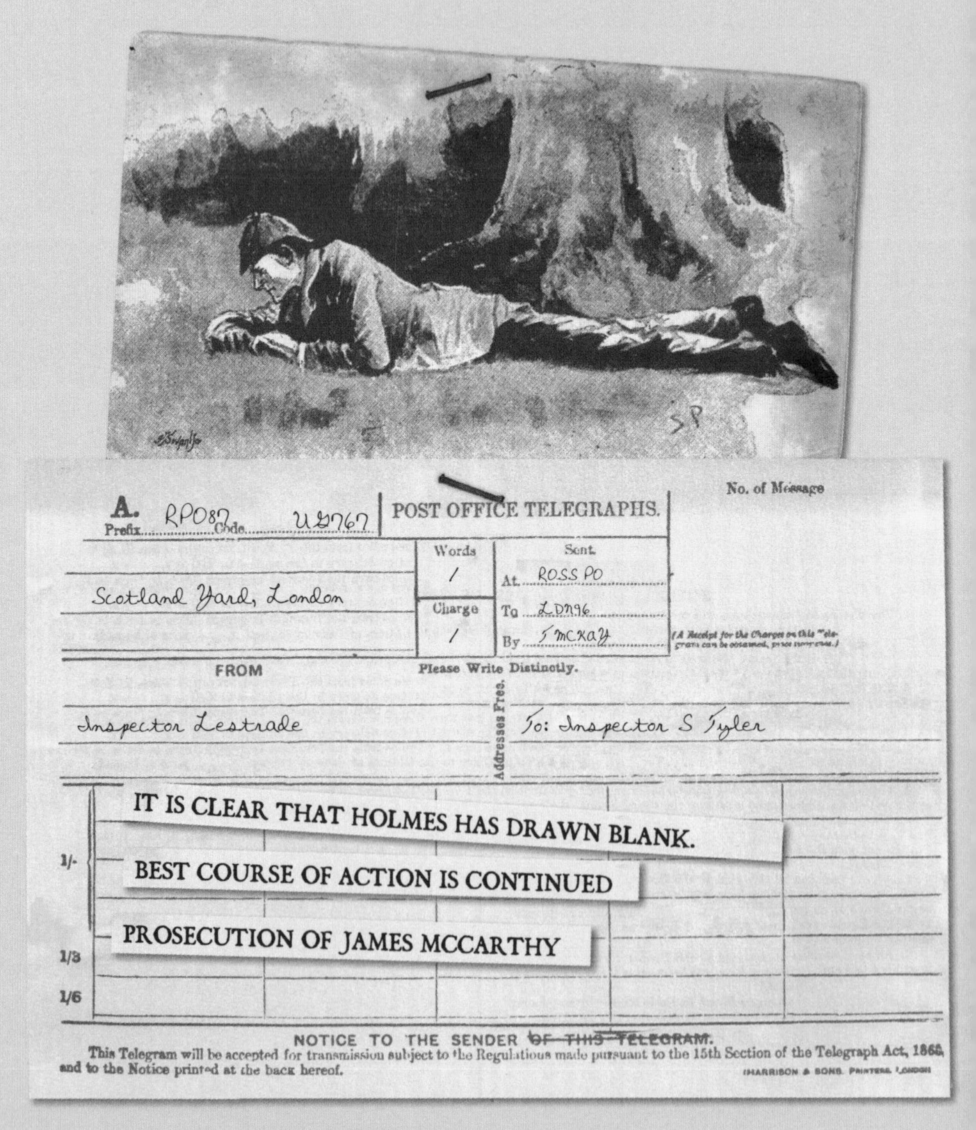

A. Prefix RPO87 Code UG767

POST OFFICE TELEGRAPHS.

No. of Message

Scotland Yard, London

Words 1

Charge 1

Sent. At ROSS PO To LD796 By S MCKAY

(A Receipt for the Charges on this Telegram can be obtained, price one penny.)

FROM

Please Write Distinctly.

Inspector Lestrade

Addresses Free.

To: Inspector S Tyler

1/-

1/3

1/6

IT IS CLEAR THAT HOLMES HAS DRAWN BLANK.
BEST COURSE OF ACTION IS CONTINUED
PROSECUTION OF JAMES MCCARTHY

NOTICE TO THE SENDER ~~OF THIS TELEGRAM.~~

This Telegram will be accepted for transmission subject to the Regulations made pursuant to the 15th Section of the Telegraph Act, 1868, and to the Notice printed at the back hereof.

(HARRISON & SONS, PRINTERS, LONDON)

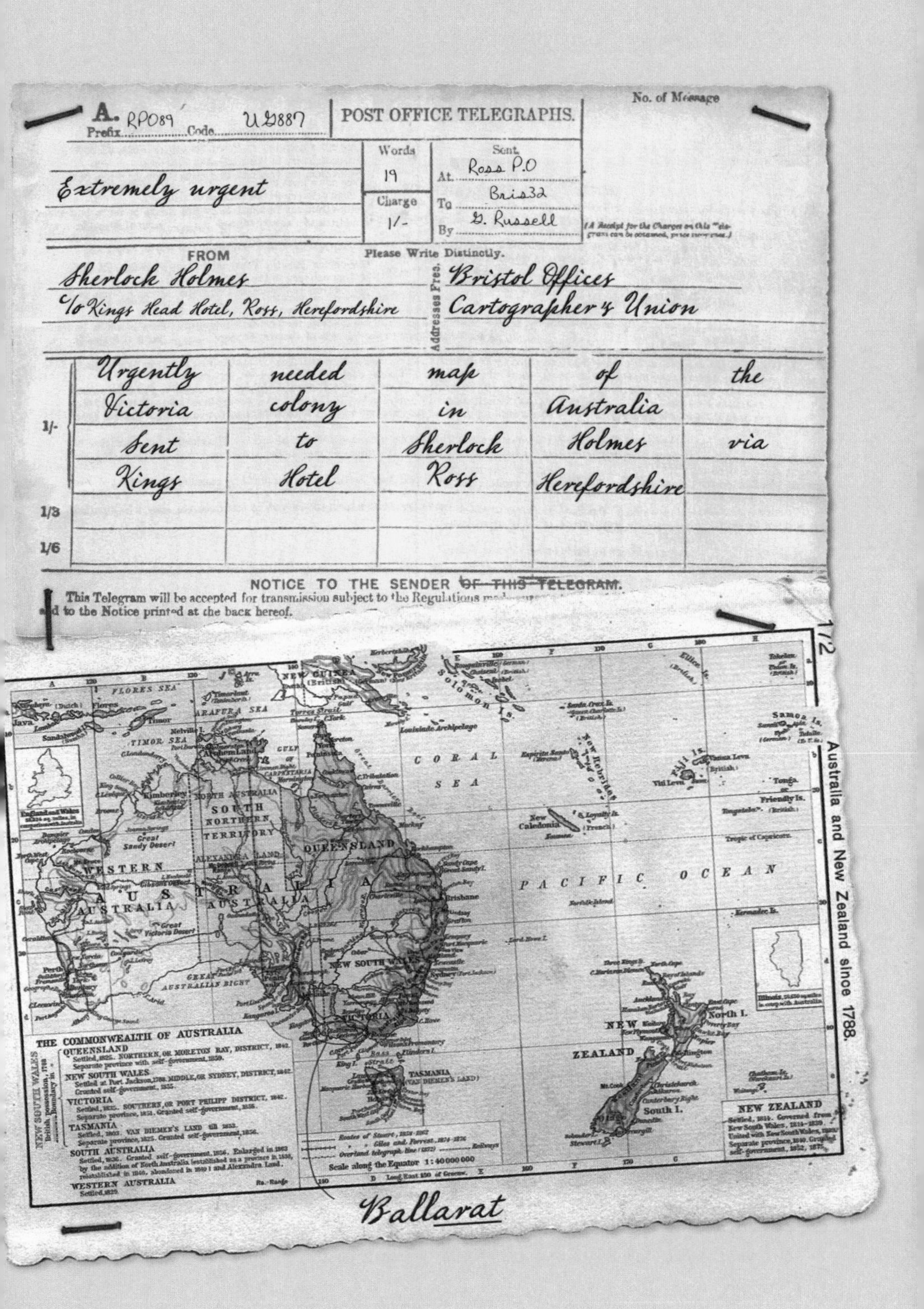

No. of Message

A. Prefix RPO89 Code U G887

POST OFFICE TELEGRAPHS.

Extremely urgent

Words 19

Charge 1/-

Sent. At Ross P.O

To Bris32

By G. Russell

(A Receipt for the Charges on this Telegram can be obtained, price one penny.)

FROM

Sherlock Holmes

C/o Kings Head Hotel, Ross, Herefordshire

Please Write Distinctly.

Addresses Pres.

Bristol Offices

Cartographer's Union

Urgently	needed	map	of	the
Victoria	colony	in	Australia	
Sent	to	Sherlock	Holmes	via
Kings	Hotel	Ross	Herefordshire	

1/-

1/3

1/6

NOTICE TO THE SENDER ~~OF THIS TELEGRAM.~~

This Telegram will be accepted for transmission subject to the Regulations made ... and to the Notice printed at the back hereof.

Holmes once again elucidated his thought processes (as usual making me feel quite dim by comparison).

He drew my attention to both the obvious matter of the call "coo-ee" and the dying man's allusion to a rat. "Coo-ee" is a distinctly Australian cry and yet it cannot possibly have been directed to his son as Charles McCarthy was unaware his son was even in the area.

Holmes exhibited a map of the Victoria colony McCarthy hailed from pointing out the location of "Ballarat".

"Approaching the problem from the assumption that everything James McCarthy has said is true are we not left with the notion that his father had been planning to meet a fellow Australian at Boscombe Pool – one to whom he called to announce his arrival. After he had been attacked he attempted to enlighten his son as to the killer, so and so from Ballarat, but his voice was week and his son only caught the last few syllables."

He further added the grey garment that James McCarthy swore was removed from the scene, the sum of these deductions leading us to an Australian from Ballarat who owned a grey cloak. Further... as the lake could only be approached by the farm or the estate, it must surely have been someone at home in the area.

The field was narrowed rather considerably!

Kings Head Hotel
Ross-On-Wye, Herefordshire

Mr Turner,

It would be to your considerable interest were you to meet me at your earliest convenience. Might I suggest you attend at my hotel The King's Head?

I assure you I wish to avoid scandal wherever possible and can only say that if you know anything of my reputation it might lead you to allow me a little of your faith.

Yours,

Sherlock Holmes

METROPOLITAN POLICE

NO. 6

OFFICIAL REPORT

Scotland Yard Station   Insp. G Lestrade Officer

Reference to papers:

You didn't know this dead man, McCarthy. He was a devil incarnate. His grip has been upon me these twenty years and has blasted my life. I'll tell you first how I came to be in his power.

It was in the early '60's at the diggings. I was a young chap then, ready to turn my hand at anything; I got among bad companions, took to drink, had no luck with my claim, took to the bush, and in a word became what you would call over here a highway robber. There were six of us, and we had a wild, free life of it, sticking up a station from time to time, or stopping the wagons on the road to the diggings. Black Jack of Ballarat was the name I went under, and our party is still remembered in the colony as the Ballarat Gang.

One day a gold convoy came down from Ballarat to Melbourne, and we lay in wait for it and attacked it. There were six troopers and six of us, so it was a close thing, but we emptied four of their saddles at the first volley. Three of our boys were killed, however, before we got the swag. I put my pistol to the head of the wagon-driver, who was this very man McCarthy. I wish to the Lord that I had shot him then, but I spared him, though I saw his wicked little eyes fixed on my face, as though to remember every feature. We got away with the gold, became wealthy men, and made our way over to England without being suspected. There I parted from my old pals and determined to settle down to a quiet and respectable life. I bought this estate, which chanced to

↑ *Signed confession of John Turner.*

be in the market, and I set myself to do a little good with my money, to make up for the way in which I had earned it. I married, too, and though my wife died young she left me my dear little Alice. Even when she was just a baby her wee hand seemed to lead me down the right path as nothing else had ever done. In a word, I turned over a new leaf and did my best to make up for the past. All was going well when McCarthy laid his grip upon me.

I had gone up to town about an investment, and I met him in Regent Street with hardly a coat to his back or a boot to his foot.

'Here we are, Jack,' says he, touching me on the arm; 'we'll be as good as a family to you. There's two of us, me and my son, and you can have the keeping of us. If you don't – it's a fine, law-abiding country is England, and there's always a policeman within hail.'

Well, down they came to the west country, there was no shaking them off, and there they have lived rent free on my best land ever since. There was no rest for me, no peace, no forgetfulness; turn where I would, there was his cunning, grinning face at my elbow. It grew worse as Alice grew up, for he soon saw I was more afraid of her knowing my past than of the police. Whatever he wanted he must have, and whatever it was I gave him without question, land, money, houses, until at last he asked a thing which I could not give. He asked for Alice.

His son, you see, had grown up, and so had my girl, and as I was known to be in weak health, it seemed a fine stroke to him that his lad should step into the whole property. But there I was firm. I would not have his cursed stock mixed with mine; not that I had any dislike to the lad, but his blood was in him, and that was enough. I stood firm. McCarthy threatened. I braved him to do his worst. We were to meet at the pool midway between our houses to talk it over.

When we went down there I found him talking with his son, so smoked a cigar and waited behind a tree until he should be alone. But as I listened to his talk all that was black and bitter in me seemed to come uppermost. He was urging his son to marry my daughter with as little regard for what she might think as if she were a slut from off the streets. It drove me mad to think that I and all that I held most dear should be in the power of such a man as this. Could I not snap the bond? I was already a dying and a desperate man. Though clear of mind and fairly strong of limb, I knew that my own fate was sealed. But my memory and my girl! Both could be saved if I could but silence that foul tongue. I did it, and would do it again. Deeply as I have sinned, I have led a life of martyrdom to atone for it. But that my girl should be entangled in the same meshes which held me was more than I could suffer. I struck him down with no more compunction than if he had been some foul and venomous beast. His cry brought back his son; but I had gained the cover of the wood, though I was forced to go back to fetch the cloak which I had dropped in my flight. That is the true story, gentlemen, of all that occurred.

John Turner

John Turner AKA "Black Jack of Ballarat"

After failing at his mining claim in the Australian colony of Ballarat, John Turner took to drink, bad company and a life of criminality. The founder of the so—called "Ballarat Gang" he made made it his business holding up wagons and provision stations.
He was to make his not inconsiderable fortune through the robbing of a gold convoy.

Investing the money, he resolved to retire from his life of crime, settling down in the quiet area of Boscombe Valley. This was not altogether successful (cross reference notes on "Boscombe Valley Murder / Charles McCarthy)

It has sometimes been my colleague's wish to avoid the mechanics of the law and this was one such case. So convinced was he of the validity of Mr John Turner's motive (and, indeed the unlikelihood of him ever proving a danger to others) that he was determined to see things resolved to everyone's mutual benefit. Therefore he made notes detailing the facts in the old man's confession for use as a last resort to save young McCarthy from the scaffold. It would never be used, Holmes presenting suitable discrepancies at the assizes that threw sufficient doubt on McCarthy's guilt.

HOLMES SAVES LIFE
BOSCOMBE VALLEY MYSTERY
SOLVED BY FAMOUS DETECTIVE

Son of Murdered Victim Set Free

The case of the murder of Mr. Charles McCarthy took an unforseen turn today. As readers may remember the ex-Australian lived in the Boscombe Valley area until his body was found on Monday the 3rd of this month. The case was presented at the assizes and it was no secret that the victim's son, James McCarthy, was expected to hang for the crime having been placed at the scene by several witnesses arguing with his father shortly before his death . The evidence against the young McCarthy seemed wholly damning until the unexpected appearance of noted consulting detective Sherlock Holmes. There can be few readers unfamiliar with the name and reputation of Mr. Holmes, certainly his name is frequently reported in connection with the solving of crime in our capital. Many will also be familiar with the dramatic reports of some of his cases as written by his colleague Dr. John Watson and reproduced in the highly popular Strand Magazine.

Mr. Holmes made short work of the evidence presented against James McCarthy, labeling it "cirumstantial and indicative of no greater fact than that James McCarthy was present at the scene of crime, something he has never denied." Mr. Holmes went on to further observe that beyond the fact that the two gentlemen had argued there was no indication of motive. James McCarthy made no claim whatsoever that he hadn't argued with his father he had simply refused to reveal the subject of that disagreement. He had done so to protect the honour of a lady for whom he had strong feelings (a lady later revealed to be the daughter of his landlord Mr. John Turner). Presenting his examination of the physical evidence, Mr. Holmes further proved that not only did James McCarthy have no motive for committing the crime but that the evidence pointed distinctly to someone else having done so. His father clearly had an appointment with someone other than his son at the time of his death (he had not known his son was even in the area), someone who had left clear physical evidence of their presence (such evidence was given in private to the bodies presiding). Much had been made of the possibility of James McCarthy's rifle stock being the blunt instrument used to perpetrate the crime, Mr. Holmes continued, not only was that unequivocally not the case now that the real weapon had been identified, but also we were supposed to imagine that James McCarthy would, in a moment of anger, put down his rifle (which would, he agreed, make a perfectly viable club) only to search out a stone with which to achieve the desired task of killing his father. The idea was, of course, preposterous, as was the entire notion that James McCarthy was anything but innocent of the crime.

Such was the conviction of Mr. Holmes and the inarguable logic and weight of his evidence that there was little surprise when James McCarthy was released as an innocent man.

↑ *Another newspaper article from our ever-present* Herefordshire Times *– this one is dated Thursday, 27 June 1889.*

THE DANCING MEN

WEDNESDAY, 27 JULY TO SATURDAY, 13 AUGUST 1898

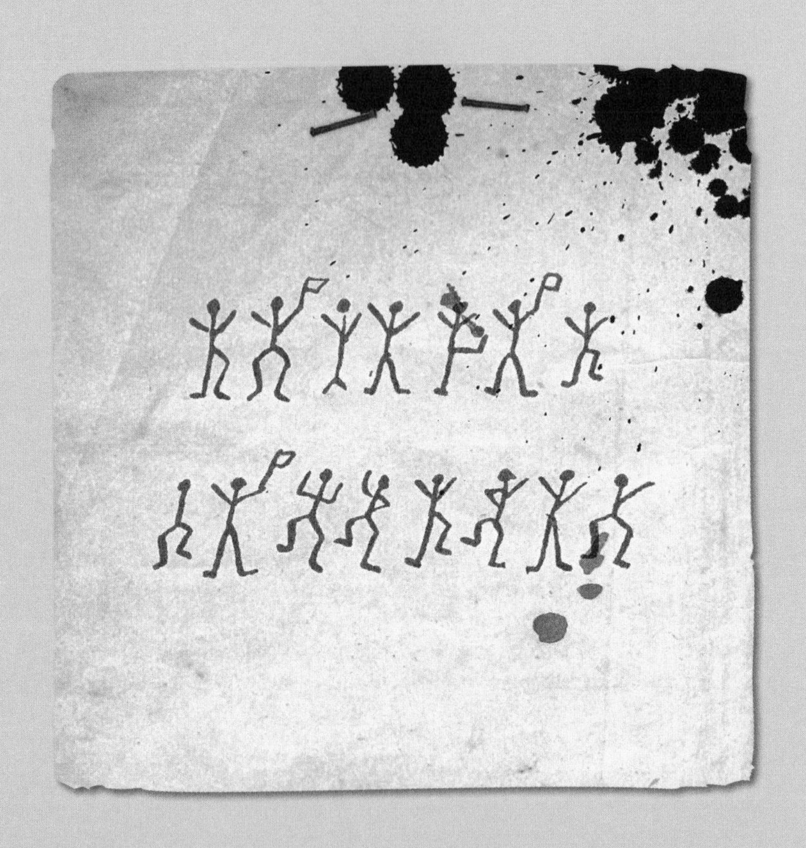

↗ *The first appearance of the mysterious "dancing men", from the note supplied by Mr Hilton Cubitt.*

Dear Mr. Holmes,

I am writing to you as a desperate man, hopeful that you may be able to help in the matter of my beloved wife.

Let me first admit that I am far from rich, though my family has resided here at Riding Thorpe in Norfolk for five centuries. I met Elsie, a young American lady, last year while visiting town for the Jubilee. You will think it mad when I tell you that I was to be married to this woman ~ of whom I knew not one jot of history ~ only one month later. If you were to meet her then you would understand, she is a woman of singular beauty.

She was most honest with me. "I have had some disagreeable associations in my life," she would say, insistent that she had nothing in herself to be ashamed of but that she would nonetheless not countenance enquiries into her past. I was to take her as a blank slate or not at all.

A year passed and we were blissfully happy but then, at the end of June, came the arrival of a letter from America.

I have no idea as to its contents (I noted the stamp before it were burnt in the fire but no more) and have not asked, though Elsie would do well to trust me I am a man of my word and I haven,t forced an enquiry. Since that letter she has known no rest, she is fearful I am sure of it.

Then, matters turn queer. Tuesday of last week I came upon the attached line of dancing figures scrawled in chalk on one of the window-sills. On mentioning it to my wife she became deeply distressed and insisted I let her see anymore that might appear. For a week none did and then, yesterday morning I found the accompanying piece of paper. I showed it to Elsie and she fainted clean away.

Clearly this is not a matter that I can allow to continue, I have no idea what these curious figures might mean but must do all in my power to find out. I shall call on you tomorrow morning so that we might discuss your initial suspicions.

Yours Faithfully,

Hilton Cubitt

↗ *Holmes had once written a monograph on decrypting ciphers, so took a great interest in what appeared to be a coded message.*

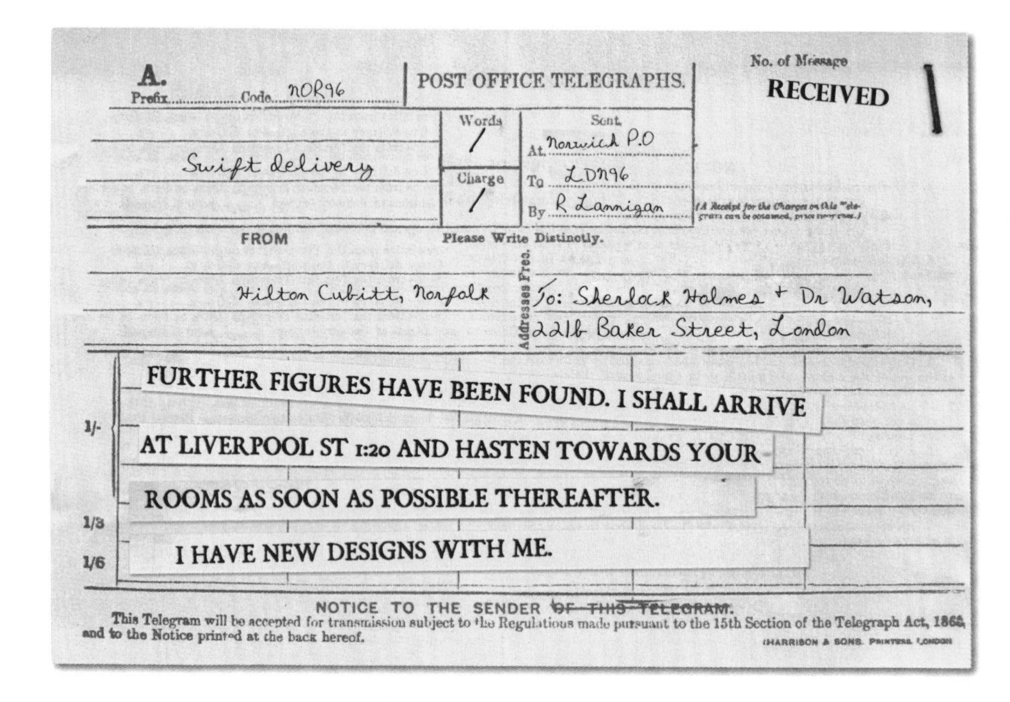

A. Prefix........ Code nOR96

POST OFFICE TELEGRAPHS.

No. of Message

RECEIVED

Swift delivery

Words 1

Charge 1

Sent At Norwich P.O

To LDN96

By R Lannigan

(A Receipt for the Charges on this Telegram can be obtained, price one penny.)

FROM

Please Write Distinctly.

Hilton Cubitt, Norfolk

Addresses Free.

To: Sherlock Holmes + Dr Watson, 221b Baker Street, London

1/-

1/3

1/6

FURTHER FIGURES HAVE BEEN FOUND. I SHALL ARRIVE AT LIVERPOOL ST 1:20 AND HASTEN TOWARDS YOUR ROOMS AS SOON AS POSSIBLE THEREAFTER. I HAVE NEW DESIGNS WITH ME.

NOTICE TO THE SENDER ~~OF THIS TELEGRAM.~~

This Telegram will be accepted for transmission subject to the Regulations made pursuant to the 15th Section of the Telegraph Act, 1868, and to the Notice printed at the back hereof.

(HARRISON & SONS. PRINTERS, LONDON

The Third Message drawn upon the black wooden door of the Tool House.

After the third message was rubbed out this fourth line of hieroglyphics appeared in the same place.

That last message was to be repeated, this time on a scrap of paper found by the sundial. Cubitt, by now quite incensed over the curious affair, resolved to lie in wait by the window, revolver in hand, determined to catch the elusive scribbler. His wife was quite beside herself at the notion and begged him to reconsider. He would not do so. Upon spotting a figure in the moonlight, Elsie Cubitt fought to stop her husband from challenging the man. Mr Cubitt was delayed long enough for the stranger to vanish, but not before he left yet one more sequence of dancing figures:

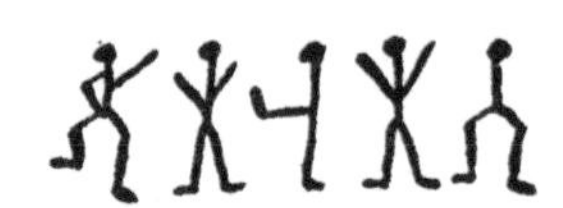

From Holmes' own sketchbook:

This message was so short I could say little with confidence except that the figure:

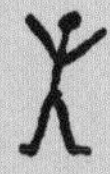

represented 'E', the most common letter in the alphabet. Out of the fifteen characters in that first message four were the same, that sort of marked predominance is the key to all successful cryptography. Twice that symbol was found to have a flag in its hand but, given the spacing between such flags I surmised that the flag told the reader where the end of a word might be rather than define a letter of its own.

Now it becomes difficult... in order of frequency the letters of the alphabet now follow this pattern: T. A. O. I. N. S. H. R. D. and L. However, T. A. O, and I are very nearly abreast of each other, and it would be an endless task to try each combination until a meaning was arrived at. We needed fresh material.

Hilton Cubitt would soon give me two other short sentences and one message, which appeared — since there was no flag — to be a single word.

I have two E's coming second and fourth in a word of five letters. It might be 'sever,' or 'lever,' or 'never.' There can be no question that the latter as a reply to an appeal is far the most probable. Accepting it as correct, we are now able to say that the symbols

stand respectively for N, V, and R.

It occurred to me that if these appeals came, as I expected, from someone who had been intimate with the lady in her early life, a combination which contained two E's with three letters between might very well stand for the name 'ELSIE.' On examination I found that such a combination formed the termination of the message which was repeated.

It was certainly some appeal to 'Elsie.' In this way I had got my L, S, and I. But what appeal could it be? There were only four letters in the word which preceded 'Elsie,' and it ended in E. Surely the word must be 'COME.' I tried all other four letters ending in E, but could find none to fit the case. So now I was in possession of C, O, and M, and I was in a position to attach the first message once more, *dividing it into words and putting dots for each symbol which was still unknown. So treated, it worked out in this fashion:*

. M . E R E . . E S L . N E .

Now the first letter can only be A, which is a most useful discovery, since it occurs no fewer than three times in this short sentence, and the H is also apparent in the second word. Now it becomes:

A M H E R E A . E S L A N E .

Or, filling in the obvious vacancies in the name:

A M H E R E A B E S L A N E Y

I had so many letters now that I could proceed with considerable confidence to the second message, which worked out in this fashion:

A . E L R I . E S

Here I could only make sense by putting T and G for the missing letters, and supposing that the name was that of some house or inn at which the writer was staying.

No. of Message

A. Prefix JN52 Code NYC23

POST OFFICE TELEGRAPHS.

Of the utmost urgency
International Wire

Words 13
Charge 10d

Sent
At Pdnt P.O
To NYC711
By D McGrath

(A Receipt for the Charges on this Telegram can be obtained, price one penny.)

Please Write Distinctly.

FROM
Sherlock Holmes
221b Baker Street, London

Addresses Fres.
Wilson Hargreaves
New York Police Bureau

A	case	of	some	merit!
Have	come	across	name	Abe
Slaney.	Someone	familiar?		

1/- 1/3 1/6

NOTICE TO THE SENDER ~~OF THIS TELEGRAM.~~
This Telegram will be accepted for transmission subject to the Regulations made pursuant to the 15th Section of the Telegraph Act, 1868, and to the Notice printed at the back hereof.

(HARRISON & SONS. PRINTERS, LONDON

No. of Message

A. Prefix JN52 Code NYC23

POST OFFICE TELEGRAPHS.

Words 13
Charge 10d

Sent
At Pdnt P.O
To NYC711
By K Lannigan

(A Receipt for the Charges on this Telegram can be obtained, price one penny.)

Of the utmost urgency
International Wire

FROM
Wilson Hargreaves
New York Police Bureau

Please Write Distinctly.

Addresses Fres.
To: Sherlock Holmes,
221b Baker Street, London

1/- 1/3 1/6

THE MOST DANGEROUS CROOK IN CHICAGO!

NOTICE TO THE SENDER ~~OF THIS TELEGRAM.~~
This Telegram will be accepted for transmission subject to the Regulations made pursuant to the 15th Section of the Telegraph Act, 1868, and to the Notice printed at the back hereof.

(HARRISON & SONS. PRINTERS, LONDON

Dear Mr. Holmes,

All is quiet here with the exception of one more message discovered, again, by the sundial:

I shall keep you posted on any further developments.

Yours Faithfully,

Hilton Cubitt

E L S I E P R E P A R E

T O M E E T T H Y

G O D

CUBITT DEATH AT THORPE MANOR

Tragedy struck last night at Riding Thorpe Manor with the violent death of Mr. Hilton Cubitt and the serious injury of his wife. Investigations are currently underway led by Inspector Martin of the Norfolk Constabulary.

The bodies of Mr. Hilton Cubitt and his wife were discovered by the house servants, aroused from their sleep by what they describe as "a terrible explosion". Moments later there followed a second noise, similar, yet quieter, to the first. Mrs King, the house cook, rushed into the room of the Cubitts' housemaid, Saunders and together they descended the stairs. The door of the study was open and they found their master lying upon his face in the centre of the room, quite dead. Near the window his wife was crouching, her head leaning against the wall. She was horribly wounded, and the side of her face was red with blood. She breathed heavily, but was incapable of saying anything. The passage, as well as the room, was full of smoke and the smell of powder. A pistol was found between them with two barrels discharged. The window was shut and fastened upon the inside. The women at once sent for the doctor and constable before, with the aid of the groom and the stable-boy, conveying their injured mistress to her room. So far as they knew, there had never been any quarrel between husband and wife. They had always looked upon them as a very united couple.

Mrs. Hilton Cubitt's injuries are said to be serious but not necessarily fatal as the bullet passed through the front of her brain. Only time will tell as to whether she regains consciousness.

The question remains: did she shoot her husband and then turn the pistol on herself? Or perhaps her husband was the aggressor and proved more successful in taking his own life? The possibility of a third person being present remains open and yet, if there were such a mysterious attacker, he has left little trace for the constabulary to follow.

NORWICH EVENING NEWS

↑ *Newspaper clipping from Saturday, 13 August.*

METROPOLITAN POLICE

NO. 8

OFFICIAL REPORT

Cubitt Residence Station —— Officer

Reference to papers:

I have nothing to hide from you, gentlemen. If I shot the man he had his shot at me, and there's no murder in that. I guess the very best case I can make for myself is the absolute naked truth. First of all, I want you gentlemen to understand that I have known this lady since she was a child. There were seven of us in a gang in Chicago, and Elsie's father was the boss of the Joint. He was a clever man, was old Patrick. It was he who invented that writing, which would pass as a child's scrawl unless you just happened to have the key to it. Well Elsie learned some of our ways. but she couldn't stand the business, and she had a bit of honest money of her own. so she gave us all the slip and got away to London. She had been engaged to me, and she would have married me, I believe, if I had taken over another profession, but she would have nothing to do with anything on the cross. It was only after her marriage to this Englishman that I was able to find out where she was. I wrote to her, but got no answer. After that I came over, and, as letters were no use, I put my messages where she could read them.

Well, I have been here a month now. I lived in that farm, where I had a room down below, and could get

↑ *A confession statement prepared by the Norfolk police, signed by Abe Slaney with an "X".*

in and out every night, and no one the wiser. I tried all I could to coax Elsie away. I knew that she read the messages, for once she wrote an answer under one of them. Then my temper got the better of me, and I began to threaten her. She sent me a letter then, imploring me to go away, and saying that it would break her heart if any scandal should come upon her husband. She said that she would come down when her husband was asleep at three in the morning, and speak with me through the end window, if I would go away afterwards and leave her in peace. She came down and brought money with her, trying to bribe me to go. This made me mad and I caught her arm and tried to pull her through the window. At that moment in rushed the husband with his revolver in his hand. Elsie had sunk down upon the floor, and we were face to face. I was heeled also, and I held up my gun to scare him off and let me get away. He fired and missed me. I pulled off almost at the same instant, and down he dropped. I made away across the garden, and as I went I heard the window shut behind me. That's God's truth, gentlemen, every word of it: and I heard no more about it until that lad came riding up with a note which made me walk in here, like a jay, and give myself into your hands.

X

(Abe Slaney)

↑ *A sketch of myself and Holmes in front of the fire in our rooms at 221b Baker Street.*

Presented to me from the excellent Sidney Paget, in honour of the anniversary of my fifth year of chronicling Holmes' adventures in The Strand Magazine.

Slaney, Abe

Member of the Patrick Gang in Chicago, a team of seven run by notorious shootist Ely Patrick.
It was Ely Patrick – father of the woman who would become Elsie Cubitt of Riding Thorpe Manor – that invented the code of the 'Dancing Men' as illustrated further in notes relating to that case (August 1898).

The code would go on to be used by all members of his gang as a method for the passing of secret messages.
Abe Slaney was condemned to death for the murder of Mr. Hilton Cubitt during the winter assizes in Norwich. His sentence was finally commuted to penal servitude due to mitigating circumstances and the certainty that Cubitt fired the first shot.

Holmes noted the fact that both servants could smell gun powder in the passage as an observation of extreme importance. He later explained that the window must have been open in order to produce a through draft with which to convey the smoke.

On checking the internal frame of the window Holmes discovered a bullet embedded in the wood.

The first "explosion" – he theorized – was the sound of two shots being fired simultaneously: Hilton Cubitt shooting at whoever was standing outside the open window and that person in turn aiming the bullet that would end Cubitt's life. Elsie Cubitt's first response after the shots were fired had been to slam and bolt the window against the attacker on the other side. Then, as the horror of the situation sunk in, she had picked up her husband's gun and attempted to take her own life.

Holmes then asked the servants whether there was an Inn known as "Elriges" close to hand. The stable-boy was familiar with the name, though it was a local farm rather than Inn. Holmes scribbled a line of figures that appeared identical to the hieroglyphs seen around Riding Thorpe, handed the message to the stable-boy and asked that he might deliver it to Elriges straightaway.

THE HOUND OF THE BASKERVILLES

SATURDAY, 31 AUGUST TO FRIDAY, 20 SEPTEMBER, 1889

We were visited by a Doctor Mortimer, a young GP with surgery in Dartmoor. The matters that brought him to our door were none other than the rather Gothic death of Sir Charles Baskerville that had been mentioned in the papers some months past. It would seem that our young doctor believed there was more to his passing than met the eye.

↑ *My initial inked sketches of the discovered paw prints left at the scene.*

Devon County Chronicle

BASKERVILLE TRAGEDY STRIKES BLOW TO COUNTY

Political Candidate Dies Suddenly, Hunt For New Heir Underway

The recent sudden death of Sir Charles Baskerville, whose name has been mentioned as the probable Liberal candidate for Mid-Devon at the next election, has cast a gloom over the county. Though Sir Charles had resided at Baskerville Hall for a comparatively short period his amiability of character and extreme generosity had won the affection and respect of all who had been brought into contact with him. In these days of *nouveaux riches* it is refreshing to find a case where the scion of an old county family which has fallen upon evil days is able to make his own fortune and to bring it back with him to restore the fallen grandeur of his line. Sir Charles, as is well known, made large sums of money in South African speculation. More wise than those who go on until the wheel turns against them, he realised his gains and returned to England with them. It is only two years since he took up his residence at Baskerville Hall, and it is common talk how large were those schemes of reconstruction and improvement which have been interrupted by his death. Being himself childless, it was his openly expressed desire that the whole countryside should, within his own lifetime, profit by his good fortune, and many will have personal reasons for bewailing his untimely end. His generous donations to local and county charities have been frequently chronicled in these columns.

The circumstances connected with the death of Sir Charles cannot be said to have been entirely cleared up by the inquest, but at least enough has been done to dispose of those rumours to which local superstition has given rise. There is no reason whatever to suspect foul play, or to imagine that death could be from any but natural causes. Sir Charles was a widower, and a man who may be said to have been in some ways of an eccentric habit of mind. In spite of his considerable wealth he was simple in his personal tastes, and his indoor servants at Baskerville Hall consisted of a married couple named Barrymore, the husband acting as butler and the wife as housekeeper. Their evidence, corroborated by that of several friends, tends to show that Sir Charles's health has for some time been impaired, and points especially to some affection of the heart, manifesting itself in changes of colour, breathlessness, and acute attacks of nervous depression. Dr James Mortimer, the friend and medical attendant of the deceased, has given evidence to the same effect.

The facts of the case are simple. Sir Charles Baskerville was in the habit every night before going to bed of walking down the famous yew alley of Baskerville Hall. The evidence of the Barrymores shows that this had been his custom. On the fourth of May Sir Charles had declared his intention of starting next day for London, and had ordered Barrymore to prepare his luggage. That night he went out as usual for his nocturnal walk, in the course of which he was in the habit of smoking a cigar. He never returned. At twelve o'clock Barrymore, finding the hall door still open, became alarmed, and, lighting a lantern, went in search of his master. The day had been wet, and Sir Charles's footmarks were easily traced down the alley. Halfway down this walk there is a gate which leads out on to the moor. There were indications that Sir Charles had stood for some little time here. He then proceeded down the alley, and it was at the far end of it that his body was discovered. One fact which has not been explained is the statement of Barrymore that his master's footprints altered their character from the time that he passed the moor-gate, and that he appeared from thence onward to have been walking upon his toes. One Murphy, a gipsy horse-dealer, was on the moor at no great distance at the time, but he appears by his own confession to have been the worse for drink. He declares that he heard cries but is unable to state from what direction they came.

No signs of violence were to be discovered upon Sir Charles's person, and though the doctor's evidence pointed to an almost incredible facial distortion – so great that Dr Mortimer refused at first to believe that it was indeed his friend and patient who lay before him – it was explained that that is a symptom which is not unusual in cases of dyspnoea and death from cardiac exhaustion. This explanation was borne out by the post-mortem examination, which showed long-standing organic disease, and the coroner's jury returned a verdict in accordance with the medical evidence. It is well that this is so, for it is obviously of the utmost importance that Sir Charles's heir should settle at the Hall and continue the good work which has been so sadly interrupted. Had the prosaic finding of the coroner not finally put an end to the romantic stories which have been whispered in connection with the affair, it might have been difficult to find a tenant for Baskerville Hall. It is understood that the next of kin is Mr. Henry Baskerville, if he be still alive, the son of Sir Charles Baskerville's younger brother. The young man when last heard of was in America, and inquiries are being instituted with a view to informing him of his good fortune.

Mr James Mortimer M.R.C.S.

Dartmoor Surgery, Old Cross Road, Grimpen.

Alexander,

You will forgive my lack of sociability these last few months I hope. I have been determined to make the journey to London many times and yet matters here continue to distract me from my plans.

I have mentioned Sir Charles Baskerville to you I'm sure. Other than Mr Frankland of Lafter Hall and the naturalist Mr Stapleton he is the only man of education for miles and I used to see a great deal of him. Yes, you will have noticed my use of the past tense, Charles Baskerville is no longer with us. Perhaps even someone as disinterested in life outside the capital as yourself may have read of this in the newspapers a few months ago? I would be surprised had you not. I enclose a clipping from our very own Devon and Country Chronicle just in case as the report is expansive in its coverage. Though it is not, as you will begin to realise, completely exhaustive of the facts.

I recall my sharing with you the legend of Baskerville Hall and its monstrous hound as your mocking laughter still comes swiftly to memory. I can only wish that Sir Charles had shared your amusement. While in every way an educated and reasoned gentleman he took the legend of his family most seriously indeed.

He would never walk the moors at night and frequently asked whether I had heard traces of an animal abroad while on my medical travels. It was a matter of absolute fact to him that a dreadful fate hung over his family (and I must confess the records he showed me of his lineage did nothing but prove him right!).

One night, some three weeks ago, I had arranged to visit Sir Charles for nothing more taxing than a sampling of his cellar and some discussion of tribal biology (a subject that interested him as deeply as I). Meeting me at the doorway I was struck by a look of such abject horror on his face that I immediately spun on my heels to follow his gaze. I glanced a shape, what I took in fact to be nothing more than a black calf, pass the head of his drive. The sighting had such a profound effect on him that I was forced to study the spot where the animal had been if only to reassure him that there was no sign of it now.

From a purely medical perspective I insisted he should get away from the moor, visit London and immerse himself in those delightful distractions that bring you such pleasure my dear Alexander! On mentioning the idea to Stapleton when we crossed paths out on the moors I found an ally in my plan and the pair of us bullied him into agreeing. It was just before he was due to

↑ *A letter from Dr Mortimer to a colleague in London detailing his thoughts on the "hound".*

leave that the tragedy occurred.

It was Barrymore, Sir Charles' butler, who discovered his body and sent immediately for me. As I had been sitting up late I was able to reach the hall within an hour of the event. I marked all the details as mentioned in the inquest - and therefore in that clipping attached - remarking his footsteps along the Yew Alley and their clear change in shape as my friend ran for his life... Sir Charles lay on his face, arms out, fingers dug into the earth. His features were convulsed with such strong emotion that I confess it was an effort to recognise the man I knew. There was no physical injury of any kind. That much was all expressed at the inquest, what was not was the trace of footprints I found near his body. They were the footprints of a gigantic hound.

Now I know you well enough to realize you will scoff at this statement but I would ask you to consider the many years we have known one another and afford me some credence. I confess fear of mockery held my tongue at the inquest - and also, more than pride, there was the reliability of the rest of my statement to consider, I would not have wished to have my other findings discounted in the wake of such an admission.

Nonetheless I have continued my own discrete investigations, consulting with others who claim to have seen something unnatural on the moor. I can hardly tell you how disturbing

I find it to have the very pillars of reason and nature challenged by such accounts. Hard-headed countrymen are in fear of the land, talking of a giant, luminous beast abroad... I gave no credence to such talk in the past but I find my skepticism grows weaker by the day. I am sure you will dismiss these thoughts, just as I would have done mere weeks ago. Perhaps you are right to do so.

I have taken the decision to consult Mr. Sherlock Holmes - I admit that your many excited reports of his exploits brought him immediately to mind - and no doubt he will dismiss any notion of the other-worldly also. If he can provide rational answers then I shall be even more indebted to his analysis. I am to meet Sir Charles' heir in a matter of days and am at a loss as to what to do with him, one hopes Mr. Holmes might prove instructive in that also. I shall, of course endeavour to call by at your practice while I am in town, you will forgive me if I make no promises until I discover the schedule of Sir Henry's arrival. I shall certain make the greatest of effort, as you might imagine my nerves have a great need for a little London air and the company of a good friend.

Yours,

James

Doctor Mortimer,

Your letter gave me considerable cause for sadness. I confess I had never met my Uncle but the realization that now I never will has weighed heavily on me. We do not miss our family until they are not there it would seem.

I have given great thought to the notion of my inheritance - as you may appreciate I have a life out here that is somewhat precious to me. Nonetheless I have no dependents and I do not for one minute think so highly of myself to believe Canada will be the worse without my farming her.

Therefore I shall resolve my affairs here and take up the Baskerville mantle just as soon as can be managed. I shall, of course, give you notice of my travel arrangements just as soon as everything is booked.

On behalf of my uncle I feel I should extend my thanks, it is clear that you were a great friend to Sir Charles and the manner with which you have gone about his affairs does his memory great credit. I look forward to making you acquaintance and can assure you that Baskerville Hall will always be a friendly place to you and your family.

Yours

Henry Baskerville

Dear Doktor Mortimer,

Thank you for your letter but I am afraid it was not reached by it's intended destination. You must forgive what is very poor English but I needs must inform you of the death of the man you wished to speak, Rodger Baskerville. He pass from the Yellow Fever many years ago. We did not know of any family, he was not a man who talked of such things.

Yours,

Dr Antonio Romero-Ruiz

A letter from Dr Antonio Romero-Ruiz informing Mr Mortimer of the death of Rodger Baskerville in 1876.

A telegram from Holmes to Watson.

A. Prefix LDN1 Code DAR23

No. of Message

Words 25 | Charge 1-/32

Sent At Plnt P.O | To GRIM11 | By P. Derry

For swift delivery

Please Write Distinctly.

FROM

Sherlock Holmes
221b Baker Street, London

Addresses Free.

John Watson
c/o Baskerville Hall, Grimpen

1/-	Please	continue	most	excellent	reports
	they	are	deeply	instructive.	I
	may	as	well	be	no
	more	than	a	few	hundred
1/3	yards	from	your	front	door!
1/6					

NOTICE TO THE SENDER ~~OF THIS TELEGRAM.~~

This Telegram will be accepted for transmission subject to the Regulations made pursuant to the 15th Section of the Telegraph Act, 1868 and to the Notice printed at the back hereof.

HARRISON & SONS, PRINTERS, LONDON

Baskerville Hall

1742

Of the origin of the Hound of the Baskervilles there have been many statements, yet as I come in a direct line from Hugo Baskerville, and as I had the story from my father, who also had it from his, I have set it down with all belief that it occurred even as is here set forth. And I would have you believe, my sons, that the same Justice which punishes sin may also most graciously forgive it, and that no ban is so heavy but that by prayer and repentance it may be removed. Learn then from this story not to fear the fruits of the past, but rather to be circumspect in the future, that those foul passions whereby our family has suffered so grievously may not again be loosed to our undoing.

Know then that in the time of the Great Rebellion (the history of which by the learned Lord Clarendon I most earnestly commend to your attention) this Manor of Baskerville was held by Hugo of that name, nor can it be gainsaid that he was a most wild, profane, and godless man.

↑ *The original document from 1742 detailing the Legend of The Hound of the Baskervilles.*

This, in truth, his neighbours might have pardoned, seeing that saints have never flourished in those parts, but there was in him a certain wanton and cruel humour which made his name a byword through the West. It chanced that this Hugo came to love (if, indeed, so dark a passion may be known under so bright a name) the daughter of a yeoman who held lands near the Baskerville estate. But the young maiden, being discreet and of good repute, would ever avoid him, for she feared his evil name. So it came to pass that one Michaelmas this Hugo, with five or six of his idle and wicked companions, stole down upon the farm and carried off the maiden, her father and brothers being from home, as he well knew. When they had brought her to the Hall the maiden was placed in an upper chamber, while Hugo and his friends sat down to a long carouse, as was their nightly custom. Now, the poor lass upstairs was like to have her wits turned at the singing and shouting and terrible oaths which came up to her from below, for they say that the words used by Hugo Baskerville, when he was in wine, were such as might blast the man who said them. At last in the stress of her fear she did that which might have daunted the bravest or most active man, for by the aid of the growth of ivy which covered (and still covers) the south wall she came down from under the eaves, and so homeward across the moor, there being three leagues betwixt the Hall and her father's farm.

It chanced that some little time later Hugo left his guests to carry food and drink--with other worse things, perchance--to his captive, and so found the cage empty and the bird escaped. Then, as it would seem, he became as one that hath a devil, for, rushing down the stairs into the dining-hall, he sprang upon the great table, flagons and trenchers flying before him, and he cried aloud before all the company that he would that very night render his body and soul to the Powers of Evil if he might but overtake the wench. And while the revellers stood aghast at the fury of the man, one more wicked or, it may be, more drunken than the rest, cried out that they should put the hounds upon her. Whereat Hugo ran from the house, crying to his grooms that they should saddle his mare and unkennel the pack, and giving the hounds a kerchief of the maid's, he swung them to the line, and so off full cry in the moonlight over the moor.

Now, for some space the revellers stood agape, unable to understand all that had been done in such haste. But anon their bemused wits awoke to the nature of the deed which was like to be done upon the moorlands. Everything was now in an uproar, some calling for their pistols, some for their horses, and some for another flask of wine. But at length some sense came back to their crazed minds, and the whole of them, thirteen in number, took horse and started in pursuit. The moon shone clear above them, and they rode swiftly abreast, taking that course which the maid must needs have taken if she were to reach her own home.

They had gone a mile or two when they passed one of the night shepherds upon the moorlands, and they cried to him to know if he had seen the hunt. And the man, as the story goes, was so crazed with fear that he could scarce speak, but at last he said that he had indeed seen the unhappy maiden, with the hounds upon her track. 'But I have seen more than that,' said he, 'for Hugo Baskerville passed me upon his black mare, and there ran mute behind him such a hound of hell as God forbid should ever be at my heels.' So the drunken squires cursed the shepherd and rode onward. But soon their skins turned cold, for there came a galloping across the moor, and the black mare, dabbled with white froth, went past with trailing bridle and empty saddle. Then the revellers rode close together, for a great fear was on them, but they still followed over the moor, though each, had he been alone, would have been right glad to have turned his horse's head. Riding slowly in this fashion they came at last upon the hounds. These, though known for their valour and their breed, were whimpering in a cluster at the head of a deep dip or goyal, as we call it, upon the moor, some slinking away and some, with starting hackles and staring eyes, gazing down the narrow valley before them.

The company had come to a halt, more sober men, as you may guess, than when they started. The most of them would by no means advance, but three of them, the boldest, or it may be the most drunken, rode forward down the goyal. Now, it opened into a broad space in which stood two of those great stones, still to be seen there, which were set by certain forgotten peoples in the days of old. The moon was shining bright upon the clearing, and there in the centre lay the unhappy maid where she had fallen, dead of fear and of fatigue. But it was not the sight of her body, nor yet was it that of the body of Hugo Baskerville lying near her, which raised the hair upon the heads of these three daredevil roysterers, but it was that, standing over Hugo, and plucking at his throat, there stood a foul thing, a great, black beast, shaped like a hound, yet larger than any hound that ever mortal eye has rested upon. And even as they looked the thing tore the throat out of Hugo Baskerville, on which, as it turned its blazing eyes and dripping jaws upon them, the three shrieked with fear and rode for dear life, still screaming, across the moor. One, it is said, died that very night of what he had seen, and the other twain were but broken men for the rest of their days.

Such is the tale, my sons, of the coming of the hound which is said to have plagued the family so sorely ever since. If I have set it down it is because that which is clearly known hath less terror than that which is but hinted at and guessed. Nor can it be denied that many of the family have been unhappy in their deaths, which have been sudden, bloody, and mysterious. Yet may we shelter ourselves in the infinite goodness of Providence, which would not forever punish the innocent beyond that third or fourth generation which is threatened in Holy Writ. To that Providence, my sons, I hereby commend you, and I counsel you by way of caution to forbear from crossing the moor in those dark hours when the powers of evil are exalted. (This from Hugo Baskerville to his sons Rodger and John, with instructions that they say nothing thereof to their sister Elizabeth.)

Hugo Baskerville

↑ *A map of the Baskerville estate and its surrounding area.*

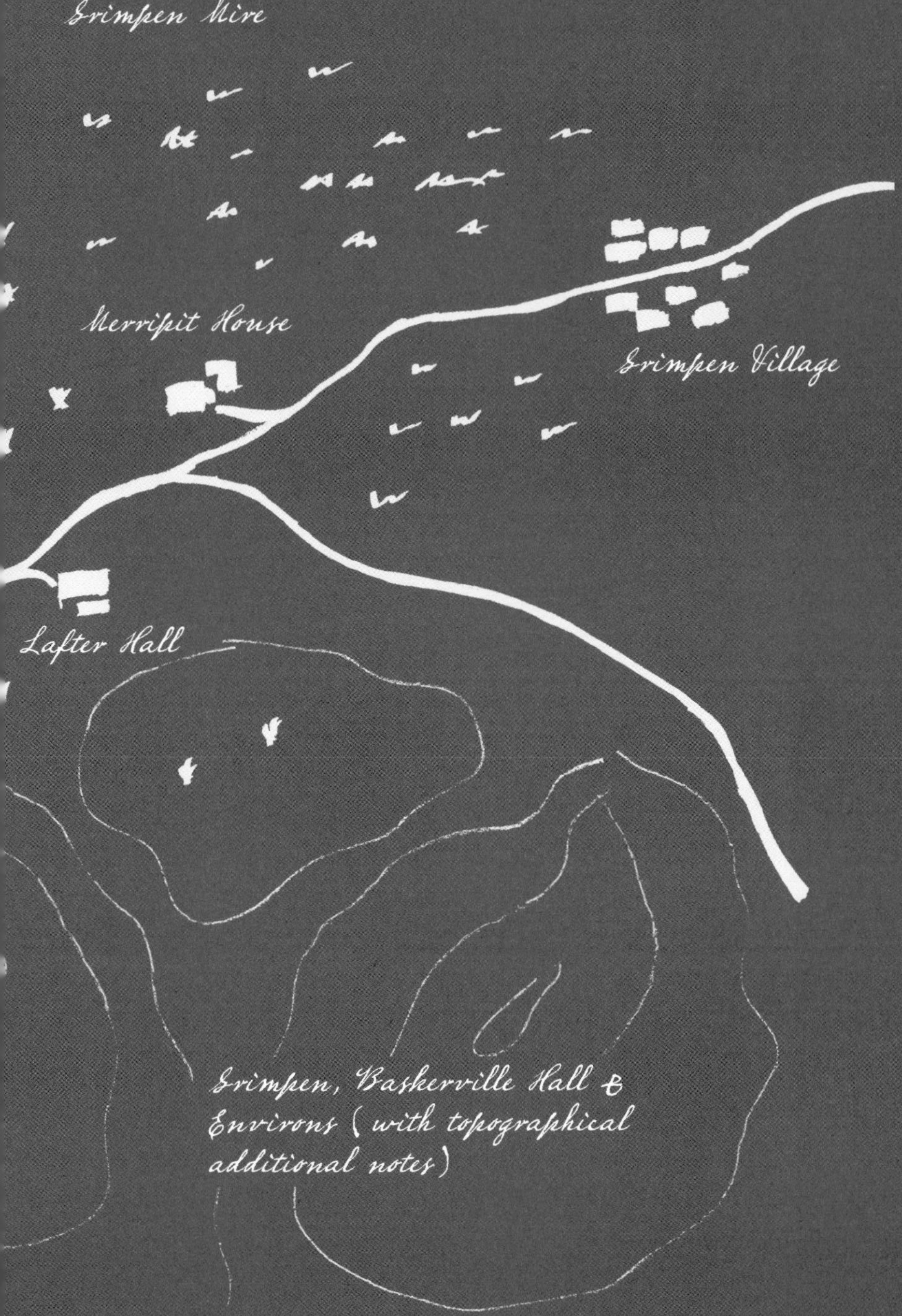

Grimpen Mire

Merripit House

Grimpen Village

Lafter Hall

Grimpen, Baskerville Hall &
Environs (with topographical
additional notes)

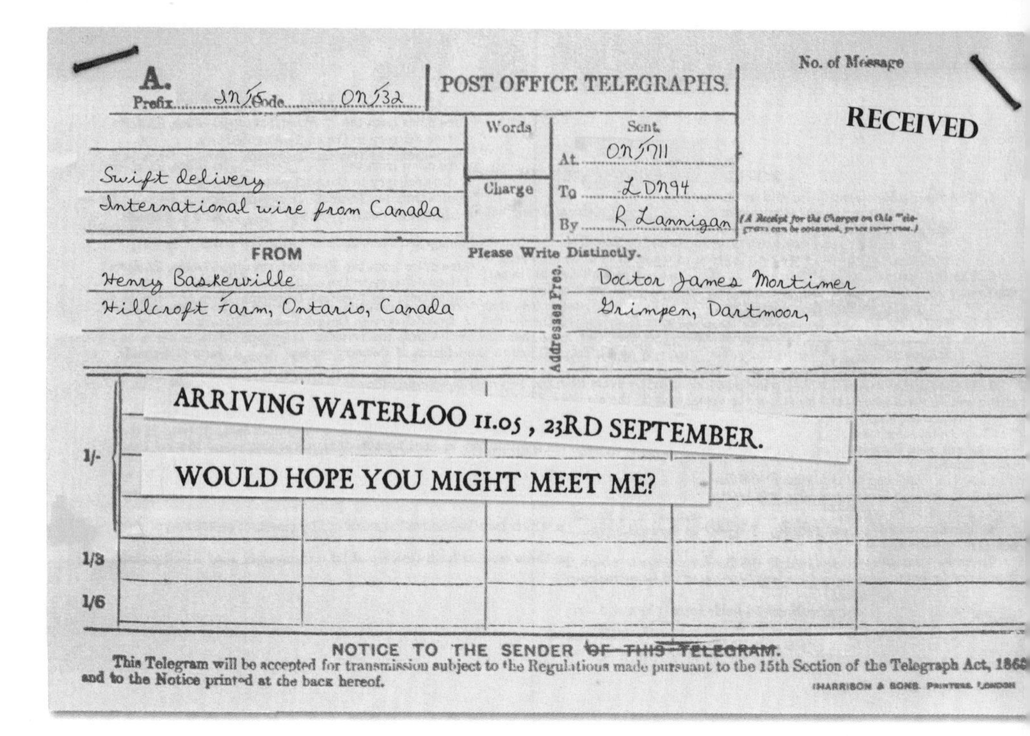

A.

Prefix JN/5 Code ON/32

POST OFFICE TELEGRAPHS.

No. of Message

RECEIVED

Words

Charge

Sent.

At ON/711

To LDN94

By R Lannigan

Swift delivery

International wire from Canada

FROM

Please Write Distinctly.

Henry Baskerville

Hillcroft Farm, Ontario, Canada

Addresses Free.

Doctor James Mortimer

Grimpen, Dartmoor,

1/-

ARRIVING WATERLOO 11.05, 23RD SEPTEMBER.

WOULD HOPE YOU MIGHT MEET ME?

1/3

1/6

NOTICE TO THE SENDER ~~OF THIS TELEGRAM.~~

This Telegram will be accepted for transmission subject to the Regulations made pursuant to the 15th Section of the Telegraph Act, 1868 and to the Notice printed at the back hereof.

HARRISON & SONS, PRINTERS, LONDON

The words were clipped from the previous day's Times *(Holmes could easily differentiate between the type fonts used by newspapers though he confesses to an error in his youth where he confused the* Leeds Mercury *with the* Western Morning News*!). The fact that the word "moor" was handwritten pointed to no other significance than that the author of the note had been unable to find the word in his paper.*

Holmes was also quick to deduce that a pair of nail scissors had been used to clip out the words: the author had needed to take two cuts in order to remove "keep away" from the article – the blades of the scissors therefore being rather short as to be unable to do the job in one.

Gum, rather than paste, had been used. The address on the envelope had been written in a rough manner but the fact that the words had been cut from The Times *(a paper seldom found anywhere but in the hands of the highly-educated) suggested to Holmes that the author had been trying to appear ill-eduated. It was also likely that they had been trying to disguise their handwriting, which would suppose that the author – and their script – might be familiar to either Sir Henry or Dr Mortimer.*

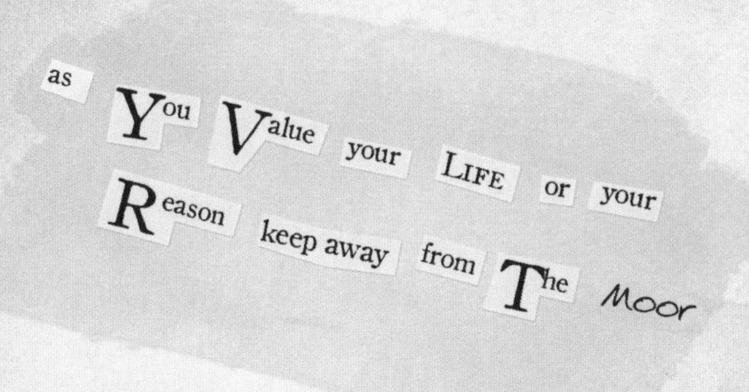

as You Value your LIFE or your Reason keep away from The moor

Sir Henry Baskerville
Northumberland Hotel
Northumberland Road London

CHARING CROSS

POSTAGE ONE PENNY

A threat? The note sent to Sir Henry Baskerville via his hotel.

The letters were not pasted in a straight manner, which suggested either carelessness or haste. Surely such a note could never be produced carelessly, begging the question as to why the author acted in haste. Any letter sent before the early morning post would have reached Sir Henry in time, so what was the cause of the author's hurry? Could it perhaps be fear of discovery? Fear of interruption?

Finally: an educated guess that the address was written in an hotel. Both pen and ink had caused the writer some difficulty, the pen spluttering twice on the same word and the ink running out three times in a short address. Holmes found it unlikely that someone's personal ink and bottle would be allowed to exist in such a state and therefore felt comfortable assuming it to be that most unreliable of tools: the hotel writing set.

Determined upon his arrival in London that he should look the part of a country squire, Sir Henry bought a great deal of clothing befitting such a gentlemen. Unfortunately, one purchase was to go astray before he even had a chance to wear it. He purchased a pair of tan boots that he left outside his hotel room so that they might be varnished. He woke in the morning to find one missing! The cleaner could offer no explanation and nor could Holmes – or at least, if he did have an idea as to why the boot had been taken he chose not to share it.

On confirming that the affair of the note had in no way altered Sir Henry's determination to take up his position we arranged to meet them for lunch and bid them farewell. No sooner had they left our rooms, however, but Holmes was grabbing me by the arm and insisting I grab my hat and coat.

A.
Prefix CAB13 Code DJB5

POST OFFICE TELEGRAPHS.

No. of Message

Of the utmost urgency

Words	Sent
25	At Plnt P.O
Charge	To WES/51
1-/32	By a. Pearce

(A Receipt for the Charges on this Telegram can be obtained, price [illegible].)

FROM
Sherlock Holmes
221b Baker Street, London

Please Write Distinctly.

Addresses Pres.
Hansom Cab Registry Office
Broadway, Westminster

	It	is	of	considerable	importance
1/-	that	I	discover	the	name
	and	address	of	the	driver
	of	cab	2704.	Please	return
1/3	same	to	221b	Baker	Street.
1/6					

NOTICE TO THE SENDER ~~OF THIS TELEGRAM.~~
This Telegram will be accepted for transmission subject to the Regulations made pursuant to the 15th Section of the Telegraph Act, 1868 and to the Notice printed at the back hereof.

HARRISON & SONS, PRINTERS, LONDON

I suggested calling out to Dr Mortimer and Sir Henry but Holmes wouldn't hear of it. The reason became clear scant minutes into our walk. Holmes was convinced that someone was following our clients and he seemed to spot the very man, a bushy-bearded cove observing from the darkness of a cab. The fellow was quick-witted however, spotting Holmes' interest almost as soon as my friend had cautiously exhibited it. With a cry he bade the driver make haste and we lost the trail of him on the busy street. My friend was quite beside himself. "If you are an honest man, Watson," he declared, "you will record this also and set it against my successes." The fact that he had managed to memorize the cab number did little to console him…

On our arrival at the Northumberland Hotel we were to find Sir Henry quite beside himself with rage, he had lost another boot! An older one this time – though that was clearly little consolation to him. Holmes seemed quite disturbed by the loss though, as usual, he refused to be drawn as to why…

After a pleasant luncheon my friend told our clients of their bearded spy. Dr Mortimer was quick to point out – though with no suggestion of malice – that the Baskerville butler, Barrymore, was in possession of a full beard. Holmes wasted no time in laying plans to determine the whereabouts of the man, sending two telegrams to Dartmoor with the specific intention of pinning down Barrymore's location.

No. of Message

A.

Prefix CaB18 Code DJB5

POST OFFICE TELEGRAPHS.

Words 6 | Charge 6d

Sent. At. Pdnt P.O To Dart87 By A Pearce

(A Receipt for the Charges on this Telegram can be obtained, price one penny.)

Deliver as soon as possible

Please Write Distinctly.

FROM

Sherlock Holmes
221b Baker Street, London

Addresses Fees.

Mr Barrymore
Baskerville Hall, Grimpen

Is	all	ready	for	
Sir	Henry?			

A.

Prefix CaB18 Code DJB5

POST OFFICE TELEGRAPHS.

No. of Message

Words 21 | Charge 1-/3d

Sent. At. Pdnt P.O To Dart87 By A Pearce

(A Receipt for the Charges on this Telegram can be obtained, price one penny.)

Urgent Notice!

Please Write Distinctly.

FROM

Sherlock Holmes
221b Baker Street, London

Addresses Fees.

The Postmaster
Grimpen

	Telegram	to	Mr	Barrymore	to
1/-	be	delivered	into	his	own
	hand.	If	absent	please	return
	wire	to	Sir	Henry	Baskerville
1/3	Northumberland	Hotel			
1/6					

NOTICE TO THE SENDER ~~OF THIS TELEGRAM.~~

This Telegram will be accepted for transmission subject to the Regulations made pursuant to the 15th Section of the Telegraph Act, 1868 and to the Notice printed at the back hereof.

(HARRISON & SONS. PRINTERS, LONDON

The Barrymore family has looked after Baskerville Hall for four generations and were provided for by Sir Charles in his will to the sum of five hundred pounds each (to Barrymore and his wife). Dr. Mortimer joked that he hoped such a thing wasn't always enough to arouse suspicion, as he had been left a thousand pounds himself.

Holmes was eager to know as to whether the servants were aware they should profit from Sir Charles' death. It would seem that Sir Charles was only too happy to talk of the provisions of his will so there can be no doubt that they knew.

The entire estate had been valued at a million pounds, the sort of gigantic sum that a man might play a desperate hand for. If something were to happen to Sir Henry it seemed the next in the line of inheritance was the Desmond family, a line of distant cousins. Mr James Desmond was an elderly clergyman in Westmoreland.

It was decided that Sir Henry needed the safe eye of a companion on his return to the moors and – with Holmes occupied in the unpleasant matter of Charles Augustus Milverton – that responsibility fell to me. I would accompany him to the family home the next day.

Driver of Cab 2704:

John Clayton, 3 Turpey Street, the Borough.
Cab is out of Shipley's Yard Nr. Waterloo Station.

Testament of Clayton:

The fare claimed to be a detective name of... none other than Sherlock Holmes!

"Holmes" hailed the cab at half-past nine in Trafalgar Square, announcing his profession as detective and offering two guineas were Clayton to drive him around all day and ask no questions.

First stop was the Northumberland where Baskerville and Mortimer were followed to Baker Street. Clayton pulled-up half-way down the street and waited the hour and a half our clients were present before - as we know - following them thereafter as far as Regent Street. Spotting me, this Bearded Imposter demanded Clayton drive to Waterloo Station at all possible haste. They made the journey in ten minutes, Clayton received his two guineas and the information that he had been driver to Sherlock Holmes.

Clayton has no worthwhile description of the man "dressed like a toff with a black beard". It is clear that his disguise achieved its aim..

→ *Pages from Holmes' notebook detailing his interview with the driver of cab 2704.*

Holmes wrote a note to me which I read on the journey to Dartmoor:

I will not bias your mind by suggesting theories or suspicions, I wish you simply to report facts in the fullest possible manner to me. You can leave me to do the theorizing.

Report anything which may seem to have a bearing, however indirect, upon the case, and especially the relations between young Baskerville and his neighbours or any fresh particulars concerning the death of Sir Charles.

I have made some inquiries myself in the last few days, but the results have, I fear, been negative. One thing only appears to be certain, and that is that Mr James Desmond, who is the next heir, is an elderly gentleman of a very amiable disposition, so that this persecution does not arise from him. I really think that we may eliminate him entirely from our calculations. There remain the people who will actually surround Sir Henry Baskerville upon the moor.

Should Sir Henry take to the thought of discharging the Barrymores as a matter of precaution I urge you to dissuade him at all costs as he could not make a greater mistake. If they are innocent it would be a cruel injustice, and if they are guilty we should be giving up all chance of bringing it home to them. No, preserve them upon our list of suspects, which currently would most pertinently seem to include: Our friend Dr Mortimer, whom I confess

I believe to be entirely honest, and his wife, of whom we know nothing. The naturalist, Stapleton, and his sister, who is said to be a young lady of attractions. There is also Mr Frankland, of Lafter Hall, another unknown factor, and one or two other neighbours. These are the folk who must be your very special study.

Finally: Keep your revolver near you night and day, and never relax your precautions.

Holmes.

Devon County Chronicle

The search for Gilbert Selden, the so-called "Notting Hill Murderer" continues three days after his escape from Princetown Gaol. Extra men have been drafted to assist in covering the area and a successful resolution is expected soon. This will be of considerable relief to those local to the moor as, despite the offer of five pounds for anyone offering information that leads to his arrest, Selden's crimes were sufficient in their atrocity that few can claim not to have been fearful for their safety since he was at large. Readers with long memories for the sensational may remember the brutal murders laid at the hands of this most unsavoury of men. It is only the clear evidence of insanity that stopped the hangman's rope.

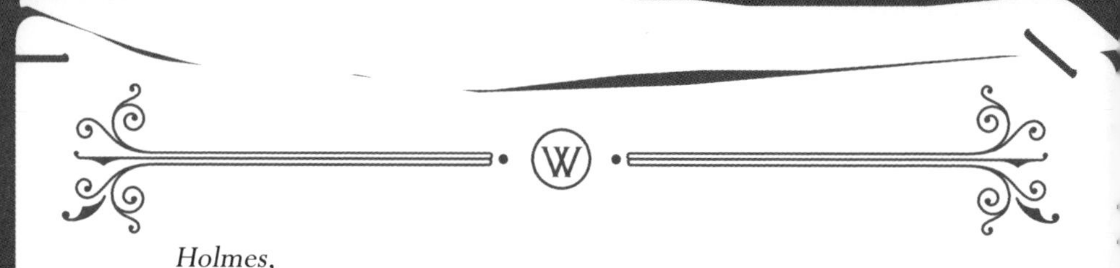

Holmes,

A quick note to let you know of the circumstances of Sir Henry and my arrival:

Firstly, as if the moor did not present enough danger to us, we arrived to the news that Selden, the Notting Hill Murderer, is loose in the area (see attached clipping)! It will be a wonder if I sleep a wink tonight.

Baskerville Hall is the very epitome of Walpole's castle... twin gothic towers rearing from a body made of ivy and cold stone. I can't say it felt particularly welcoming to either Sir Henry or me.

Dr. Mortimer left us at the gates, wishing to return home to his wife and so Sir Henry and I were left to the attentions of Barrymore and his wife. Both have been most attentive and yet it would seem they wish to leave service. Barrymore has explained that they were both close to Sir Charles and neither would feel comfortable within the walls of the Hall now that he has gone. They have promised to stay on until Sir Henry can make alternative arrangements but have pledged to use the money Sir Charles left them to set up in business.

Sir Henry did his best to present a sympathetic front and left for bed early claiming that he had no doubt the morning would find the whole situation seem more cheery. He is certainly a stout fellow and I confess I take a great liking to his company.

I had intended to leave this note there, Holmes, but I have just drawn the writing materials close having heard the most uncontrollable sobbing. It is the middle of the night (and, as predicted I have yet to rest!) and the sound was most certainly coming from within the house. I can only assume it was from the lips of Mrs. Barrymore. All is silent now and I shall attempt once more to sleep.

One last word from me then I shall drop this letter into the post for you. I inquired of Sir Henry over breakfast as to whether he had heard the noise during the night and he admitted that he had (though, being on the edge of sleep, had dismissed it as a dream). He immediately inquired of Barrymore who insisted that the noise had not come from his wife. Later I saw Mrs. Barrymore and her eyes told the lie of her husband, they were puffy and pink, most surely it had been her that had cried in the night. Why would he risk such easy detection by lying I wonder? Already it is Barrymore that carries the heavy cloak of suspicion I feel. While at the post office I shall check that our telegram definitely found his hands.

More soon.

John Watson

↓ *Sir Henry and I arrived at Baskerville Hall.*

↑ *I met the naturalist Stapleton on the moor...*

BASKERVILLE HALL
13 October

My Dear Holmes,

My previous letters and telegrams have kept you pretty well up to date as to all that has occurred in this most God-forsaken corner of the world. The longer one stays here the more does the spirit of the moor sink into one's soul, its vastness, and also its grim charm. When you are once out upon its bosom you have left all traces of modern England behind you, but on the other hand you are conscious everywhere of the homes and the work of the prehistoric people. On all sides of you as you walk are the houses of these forgotten folk, with their graves and the huge monoliths which are supposed to have marked their temples. As you look at their grey stone huts against the scarred hillsides you leave your own age behind you, and if you were to see a skin-clad, hairy man crawl out from the low door fitting a flint-tipped arrow on to the string of his bow, you would feel that his presence there was more natural than your own. The strange thing is that they should have lived so thickly on what must always have been most unfruitful soil. I am no antiquarian, but I could imagine that they were some unwarlike and harried race who were forced to accept that which none other would occupy.

All this, however, is foreign to the mission on which you sent me and will probably be very uninteresting to your severely practical mind. I can still remember your complete indifference as to whether the sun moved round the earth or the earth round the sun. Let me, therefore, return to the facts concerning Sir Henry Baskerville.

If you have not had any report within the last few days it is

↑ *My first full report to Holmes from his time at Baskerville Hall.*

because up to today there was nothing of importance to relate. Then a very surprising circumstance occurred, which I shall tell you in due course. But, first of all, I must keep you in touch with some of the other factors in the situation.

One of these, concerning which I have said little, is the escaped convict upon the moor. There is strong reason now to believe that he has got right away, which is a considerable relief to the lonely householders of this district.
A fortnight has passed since his flight, during which he has not been seen and nothing has been heard of him. It is surely inconceivable that he could have held out upon the moor during all that time. Of course, so far as his concealment goes there is no difficulty at all. Any one of these stone huts would give him a hiding-place. But there is nothing to eat unless he were to catch and slaughter one of the moor sheep. We think, therefore, that he has gone, and the outlying farmers sleep the better in consequence.

We are four able-bodied men in this household, so that we could take good care of ourselves, but I confess that I have had uneasy moments when I have thought of the Stapletons. They live miles from any help. There are one maid, an old manservant, the sister, and the brother, the latter not a very strong man. They would be helpless in the hands of a desperate fellow like this Notting Hill criminal, if he could once effect an entrance. Both Sir Henry and I were concerned at their situation, and it was suggested that Perkins the groom should go over to sleep there, but Stapleton would not hear of it.

The fact is that our friend, the baronet, begins to display a considerable interest in our fair neighbour. It is not to be wondered at, for time hangs heavily in this lonely spot to an active man like him, and she is a very fascinating and beautiful woman. There is something tropical and exotic about her which forms a singular contrast to her cool and unemotional brother. Yet he also gives the idea of hidden fires. He has certainly a very marked influence over her, for I have seen her continually glance at him as she talked as if seeking approbation for what she said. I trust that he is kind to her. There is a dry glitter in his eyes, and a firm set of his thin lips, which goes with a positive and possibly a harsh nature. You would find him an interesting study.

He came over to call upon Baskerville on that first day, and the very next morning he took us both to show us the spot where the legend of the wicked Hugo is supposed to have had its origin. It was an excursion of some miles across the moor to a place which is so dismal that it might have suggested the story. We found a short valley between rugged tors which led to an open, grassy space flecked over with the white cotton grass. In the middle of it rose two great stones, worn and sharpened at the upper end, until they looked like the huge corroding fangs of some monstrous beast. In every way it corresponded with the scene of the old tragedy. Sir Henry was much interested and asked Stapleton more than once whether he did really believe in the possibility of the interference of the supernatural in the affairs of men. He spoke lightly, but it was evident that he was very much in earnest. Stapleton was guarded in his replies, but it was easy to see that he said less than he might, and that he would not express his whole opinion out of consideration for the feelings of the baronet. He told us of similar cases, where families had suffered from some evil influence, and he left us with the impression that he shared the popular view upon the matter.

On our way back we stayed for lunch at Merripit House, and it was there that Sir Henry made the acquaintance of Miss Stapleton. From the first moment that he saw her he appeared to be strongly attracted by her, and I am much mistaken if the feeling was not mutual. He referred to her again and again on our walk home, and since then hardly a day has passed that we have not seen something of the brother and sister. They dine here tonight, and there is some talk of our going to them next week. One would imagine that such a match would be very welcome to Stapleton, and yet I have more than once caught a look of the strongest disapprobation in his face when Sir Henry has been paying some attention to his sister. He is much attached to her, no doubt, and would lead a lonely life without her, but it would seem the height of selfishness if he were to stand in the way of her making so brilliant a marriage. Yet I am certain that he does not wish their intimacy to ripen into love, and I have several times observed that he has taken pains to prevent them from being tête-à-tête. By the way, your instructions to me never to allow Sir Henry to go out alone will become very much more onerous if a love affair were to be added to our other difficulties. My popularity would soon suffer if I were to carry out your orders to the letter.

The other day – Thursday, to be more exact – Dr. Mortimer lunched with us. He has been excavating a barrow at Long Down, and has got a prehistoric skull which fills him with great joy. Never was there such a single-minded enthusiast as he! The Stapletons came in afterwards, and the good doctor took us all to the Yew Alley, at Sir Henry's request, to show us exactly how everything occurred upon that fatal night. It is a long, dismal walk, the Yew Alley, between two high walls of clipped hedge, with a narrow band of grass upon either side. At the far end is an old tumble-down summer-house. Half-way down is the moor-gate, where the old gentleman left his cigar-ash. It is a white wooden gate with a latch. Beyond it lies the wide moor. I remembered your theory of the affair and tried to picture all that had occurred. As the old man stood there he saw something coming across the moor, something which terrified him so that he lost his wits, and ran and ran until he died of sheer horror and exhaustion. There was the long, gloomy tunnel down which he fled. And from what? A sheep-dog of the moor? Or a spectral hound, black, silent, and monstrous? Was there a human agency in the matter? Did the pale, watchful

Barrymore know more than he cared to say? It was all dim and vague, but always there is the dark shadow of crime behind it.

One other neighbour I have met since I wrote last. This is Mr. Frankland, of Lafter Hall, who lives some four miles to the south of us. He is an elderly man, red-faced, white-haired, and choleric. His passion is for the British law, and he has spent a large fortune in litigation. He fights for the mere pleasure of fighting and is equally ready to take up either side of a question, so that it is no wonder that he has found it a costly amusement. Sometimes he will shut up a right of way and defy the parish to make him open it. At others he will with his own hands tear down some other man's gate and declare that a path has existed there from time immemorial, defying the owner to prosecute him for trespass. He is learned in old manorial and communal rights, and he applies his knowledge sometimes in favour of the villagers of Fernworthy and sometimes against them, so that he is periodically either carried in triumph down the village street or else burned in effigy, according to his latest exploit. He is said to have about seven lawsuits upon his hands at present, which will probably swallow up the remainder of his fortune and so draw his sting and leave him harmless for the future. Apart from the law he seems a kindly, good-natured person, and I only mention him because you were particular that I should send some description of the people who surround us. He is curiously employed at present, for, being an amateur astronomer, he has an excellent telescope, with which he lies upon the roof of his own house and sweeps the moor all day in the hope of catching a glimpse of the escaped convict. If he would confine his energies to this all would be well, but there are rumours that he intends to prosecute Dr. Mortimer for opening a grave without the consent of the next-of-kin, because he dug up the Neolithic skull in the barrow on Long Down. He helps to keep our lives from being monotonous and gives a little comic relief where it is badly needed.

And now, having brought you up to date on the escaped convict, the Stapletons, Dr. Mortimer, and Frankland, of Lafter Hall, let me end on that which is most important and tell you more about the Barrymores, and especially about the surprising development of last night.

First of all about the test telegram, which you sent from London in order to make sure that Barrymore was really here. I have already explained that the testimony of the postmaster shows that the test was worthless and that we have no proof one way or the other. I told Sir Henry how the matter stood, and he at once, in his forthright fashion, had Barrymore up and asked him whether he had received the telegram himself. Barrymore said that he had.

"Did the boy deliver it into your own hands?" asked Sir Henry. Barrymore looked surprised, and considered for a little time.

"No," said he, "I was in the box-room at the time, and my wife brought it up to me."

"Did you answer it yourself?"

"No; I told my wife what to answer and she went down to write it."

In the evening he recurred to the subject of his own accord.

"I could not quite understand the object of your questions this morning, Sir Henry," said he. "I trust that they do not mean that I have done anything to forfeit your confidence?"

Sir Henry had to assure him that it was not so and pacify him by giving him a considerable part of his old wardrobe, the London outfit having now all arrived.

Mrs. Barrymore is of interest to me. She is a heavy, solid person, very limited, intensely respectable, and inclined to be puritanical. You could hardly conceive a less emotional subject. Yet I have told you how, on the first night here, I heard her sobbing bitterly, and since then I have more than once observed traces of tears upon her face. Some deep sorrow gnaws ever at her heart. Sometimes I wonder if she has a guilty memory which haunts her, and sometimes

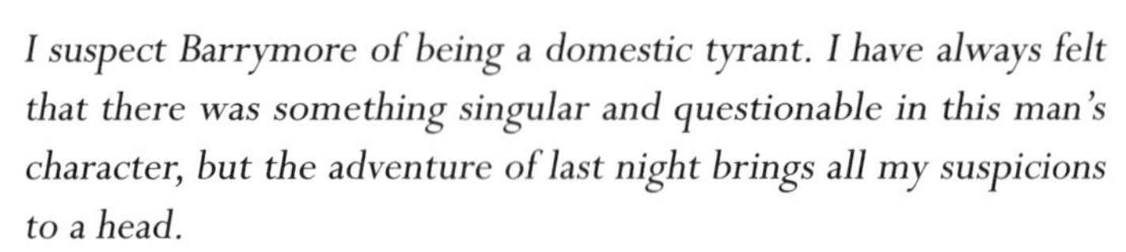

I suspect Barrymore of being a domestic tyrant. I have always felt that there was something singular and questionable in this man's character, but the adventure of last night brings all my suspicions to a head.

And yet it may seem a small matter in itself. You are aware that I am not a very sound sleeper, and since I have been on guard in this house my slumbers have been lighter than ever. Last night, about two in the morning, I was aroused by a stealthy step passing my room. I rose, opened my door, and peeped out. A long black shadow was trailing down the corridor. It was thrown by a man who walked softly down the passage with a candle held in his hand. He was in shirt and trousers, with no covering to his feet. I could merely see the outline, but his height told me that it was Barrymore. He walked very slowly and circumspectly, and therewas something indescribably guilty and furtive in his whole appearance.

I have told you that the corridor is broken by the balcony which runs round the hall, but that it is resumed upon the farther side. I waited until he had passed out of sight and then I followed him. When I came round the balcony he had reached the end of the farther corridor, and I could see from the glimmer of light through an open door that he had entered one of the rooms. Now, all these rooms are unfurnished and unoccupied, so that his expedition became more mysterious than ever. The light shone steadily as if he were standing motionless. I crept down the passage as noiselessly as I could and peeped round the corner of the door.

Barrymore was crouching at the window with the candle held against the glass. His profile was half turned towards me, and his face seemed to be rigid with expectation as he stared out into the blackness of the moor. For some minutes he stood watching intently. Then he gave a deep groan and with an impatient gesture he put out the light. Instantly I made my way back to my room, and very shortly came the stealthy steps passing once more upon their return journey. Long afterwards when I had fallen into a light sleep I heard a key turn somewhere in a lock, but I could not tell whence the sound came. What it all means I cannot guess, but there is some secret business going on in this house of gloom which sooner or later we shall get to the bottom of. I do not trouble you with my theories, for you asked me to furnish you only with facts. I have had a long talk with Sir Henry this morning, and we have made a plan of campaign founded upon my observations of last night. I will not speak about it just now, but it should make my next report interesting reading.

John Watson

↑ *I also made the acquaintance of his sister on the grim landscape of the moors.*

On checking with the postmaster it became clear that our telegram was not, as promised, delivered directly into Barrymore's hands. Mrs Barrymore had taken it from the postmaster's boy explaining that her husband was in the loft. For all we knew he could have been in London all the time.

On my return from Grimpen I met Stapleton, the naturalist, who was quick to warn me of the dangers of the moor, most particularly the treacherous Grimpen Mire that had claimed the life of many wild horses and, indeed, hikers. He also expounded his theory that Sir Charles had died a victim of his own credulity, perhaps pursued by a stray animal that his belief in the legend of his family turned into something altogether more potent.

While Stapleton's attention was distracted by a passing moth I was engaged by the man's sister who embarrassingly mistook me for Sir Henry. "Go back!" she said, "Go straight back to London, instantly!" She hid all signs of her entreaty upon the return of her brother who introduced me, revealing her error in assumption and embarrassing her rather. We took tea and later, when again afforded privacy, she apologized and insisted that her comments had been through her own belief in the legend of the Baskervilles and that I wasn't to mention them to her brother as he considered such belief foolish and was determined to see the hall occupied for the good of the area.

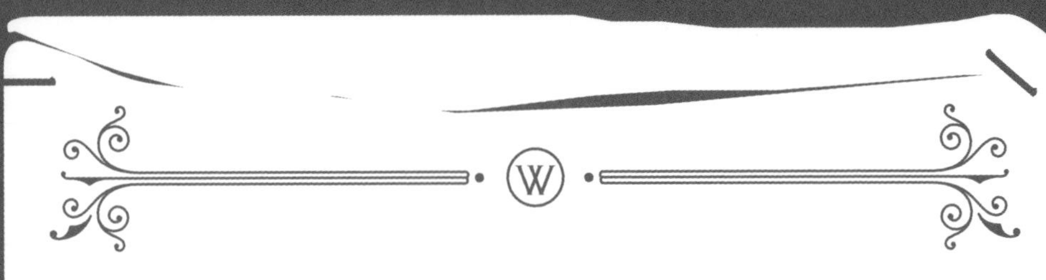

Holmes,

Sir Henry was in a black mood this morning after the excitements of the night and I can't say my humour was much different. It is clear to me that the man we saw on the moor last night is a stranger to us, as I am familiar enough with the neighbours by now to be assured it wasn't them. The idea that we are therefore no closer to understanding this matter is disturbing at the very least.

There was a brief scene at breakfast with Barrymore over the matter of our seeking out Selden. He feels that we have acted dishonourably as he admitted of his wife's brother's presence of his own free will and considers our willingness to report all to the police a poor response to his honesty. He has sworn that Selden will be no danger to anyone and further disclosed their plans to put him on a ship to Central America in the next couple of days. After some consideration – and bearing in mind what we have heard of Selden from his sister – Sir Henry and I were inclined to let that be an end to the matter. Barrymore, now in a fit of good humour, wished to repay us with some information he possessed regarding the death of Sir Charles (and it is this more than anything else that I was determined to pass on to you). He believes he knows why Sir Charles was waiting at the gate at that late hour: it was to meet a woman.

Barrymore had noticed a letter arriving from Coombe Tracey addressed to Sir Charles by a woman's hand. He claims to have dismissed the correspondence from his mind until, a couple of weeks ago, a scrap of what he is convinced was the same letter was found by his wife in the hearth of Sir Charles' office. The postscript was still readable:

"Please, please, as you are a gentleman, burn this letter, and be at the gate by ten o clock." Beneath it were signed the initials L. L.

Of course both Sir Henry and I were baffled as to why Barrymore hadn't mentioned this earlier. The manservant claims he could see no good coming from the information, he was fearful of harming Sir Charles' reputation and, of course, by the time of the discovery he and his wife had more than enough problems of their own to contend with.

Sir Henry is determined that we should try and trace this "L.L." from Coombe Tracey for surely she might answer a good many of our questions. He asked me specifically to pass the event on – as I naturally would have anyway – as he remains ever hopeful that you might come down to join us. I can tell from your brief notes that matters with the blackmailer are complex and distract you from our situation here but I must confess I share Sir Henry's wish to have you down here, things grow murkier by the day and I am not so proud a man as to deny that having you here would certainly help illuminate matters.

Barrymore was to provide some further small interest as I later asked him when he had last seen Selden. Apparently he had had no contact, though had left out some food a couple of days ago that had certainly been collected. "Then that proves he is still abroad." I commented to which Barrymore surprised me by noting that "the other man" might have taken the food. It seems Barrymore has known for some time that there is someone else on the moor, Selden having mentioned it to him over a week ago. Apparently he makes his residence in the Neolithic village and has a lad from the village bring him food…

So, we have two mysteries to solve… the identity of "L.L." and the stranger on the moor…

I swear that by next time we speak I shall have done everything within my power to get to the heart of both.

Yours

John Watson

I consulted Dr Mortimer as to the identity of a woman in the area with initials "L.L." and he was quick to furnish me with the only lady who came to mind: Laura Lyons, daughter of none other than Frankland of Lafter Hall (she lost her surname and something of her reputation after marrying an artist who deserted almost as soon as the ink had dried on the certificate). It would seem that her father would have no more to do with her and only the charity of others had enabled her to set up a typing office in Coombe Tracey.

My meeting was, of course, delicate... I could only prevail upon Mrs. Lyons that my questions sought to avoid the possibility of a public scandal rather than create one. She confessed to great admiration for Sir Charles, it was largely due to his generosity – and that of a handful of others, Stapleton for one – that she had managed to survive financially after her husband abandoned her. She confessed to writing to Sir Charles on a couple of times but only to express her gratitude. When I declared that I knew that not to be altogether true, that in fact

she had written to him on the very day of his death (and with a request to meet him) she near fainted away with shock.

"Is there no such thing as a gentleman?" she asked, in reference to her insistence that Sir Charles should burn the letter. I explained that he had done so but sufficient had remained legible to have caused this interview.

Of course she could do little else but admit to the letter now that the facts were known. It seemed that she had written to Sir Charles as her errant husband had contacted her offering the reward of a divorce if she were to give him money. So desperate was she to escape her situation that she wrote to arrange a meeting in the hope that she might convince him to pay the scoundrel Lyons off. She insisted that she had not kept the appointment, however, as she had received the money she needed from elsewhere (though refused to be drawn as to the source). I left her to her work but could not shake the impression that there must be more to her story than she claimed.

Once again it would seem that the determination of Mr Franklin of Lafter Hall, Grimpen has paid off within the law courts. Mr. Franklin's exploits will be familiar to most readers as he makes something of a business involving himself in the tribulations of local law. Many will remember, in particular, the legal loophole that saw Sir John Morland sued for trespass when shooting in his own warren.

Today brings news of two more success for Mr. Frankland. The first is the establishment of a right of way through the centre of Mr. Middleton's property (also of the Grimpen area). It is believed that a path, free for all to use, now lies no more than one hundred yards from the gentleman's front door. Mr. Middleton refused to give comment for print but was clearly most aggravated by the news, as are the people of Fernworthy as Mr. Frankland's second success has seen their local wood closed to visitors. The area was popular for picnicking but was not actually public land and is now to be fenced off to protect against trespass.

Mr. Frankland has commented: "This is a red-letter day for the law! No longer shall she be flouted while I live on to protect her honour!"

↑ *Mention of Frankland's latest legal successes in the local paper.*

On my return journey to Baskerville Hall I was waylaid by Frankland who was stood by the side of the road. Despite my slight indisposition towards the man after learning how he mistreated his daughter, I could hardly ignore his invitation to take a glass of wine in his company. He was in a most celebratory mood after learning of a double win in the law courts.

Once Frankland had ceased crowing about his successes he spent a little time berating the local constabulary for not following his best interests. I confess I was searching for an excuse to leave until he mentioned knowing something that would be of great interest to the police but that he would take great pleasure in keeping to himself. I attempted to hide my interest, goading him with the assumption that it was a trifling matter such as poaching that he was privy to. This had the desired effect as he boasted knowing of no less a piece of information than the location of the escaped convict on the moor.

I worried for Barrymore but then Frankland clarified his boast: "You'll be surprised to hear that his food is taken to him by a child. I see him every day through my telescope upon the roof. He passes along the same path at the same hour, and to whom should he be going except to the convict?"

By great chance he happened to espy movement on the hillside and was able to prove his supposition by offering me the eyeglass. I watched the young lad crest the hill and vanish in the direction of the Neolithic village. Could it be I had tracked my elusive stranger?

I approached the stone village as cautiously as Stapleton might approach a butterfly. There was the trace of a worn path leading through the boulders to a dilapidated opening which might serve as a door. I withdrew my revolver and stepped inside, nerves tingling... The place was empty, though there were certainly signs of life: blankets and waterproofs, the remnants of a fire. A litter of tins showed that the place had been occupied for some considerable time. I noticed the recently delivered food parcel, recognizing it from the grip of the boy I had spotted through Frankland's telescope. Beneath it lay a sheet of paper with a roughly-scrawled message...

Clearly every move I had made had been traced by this stranger – or his agent – I resolved to wait and discover this man's identity. Finally, as dusk settled, his shadow settled across the light of the opening and I cocked my revolver.

"It's a lovely evening, my dear Watson," said a well-known voice. "I rather think that you will be more comfortable outside than in." It was Holmes!

My friend had been here all along it transpired, my reports of events being redirected to him as he observed – unknown by all – able to go about his investigation with utter anonymity. I confess I was slighted in the first instance but he was quick to take me into his confidence now that we were reunited.

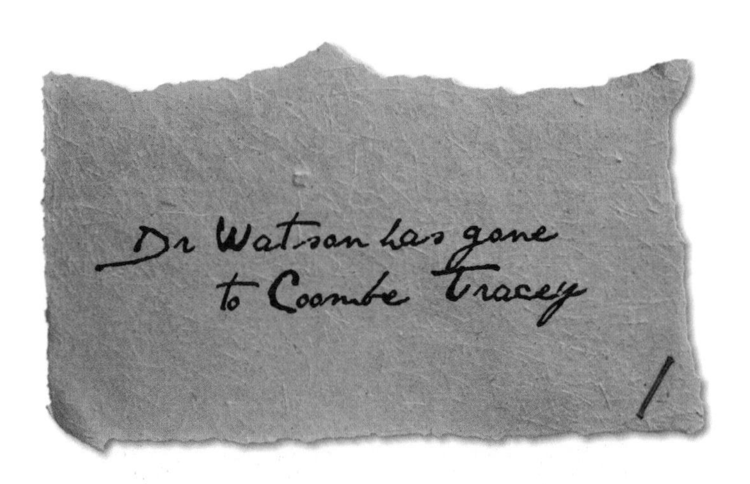
Dr Watson has gone
to Coombe Tracey

Dear Mr. Holmes,

I confess your enquiry had me quite dumbfounded until your mention of etymology rang a bell. There certainly was a schoolmaster who fits your description though his name was not Stapleton it was Vandeleur. It would not be altogether surprising for the gentleman to have changed his name, however as he left our profession under a considerable cloud. His school was a small affair in a village called Millington just outside York. Reports vary – and far be it from me to be the spreader of gossip – but what we do know is that three of his pupils died. He claimed them to be the victims of illness, an epidemic that had raged through his charges before the best efforts of the nurse could hold it in check. Perhaps that is all it was, though certainly the authorities remain unconvinced otherwise they would hardly be so eager to make his reacquaintance.

Certainly if you know the whereabouts of the gentleman then the police will be pleased to hear from you but then – given your reputation, Mr. Holmes, which reaches even our provincial ears – I'm sure they usually are. I enclose both a photograph and letter from a relative of one of Mr. Vandeleur's charges in the hope that they should provide the information you need in order to confirm the gentleman's identity – and that of course of his wife.

Yours,
Sheila Walker

That last sentence beared up to re-reading... His wife? As so often the way my friend's investigations challenged much that I had cherished as fact. Stapleton was not the man I imagined, nor was the woman he lived with his sister, as had been claimed. Holmes was close to the proof he needed to stop Stapleton's plans but we needed to play a cautious game a little while longer, he insisted. As if mocking our intentions our conversation was disturbed by the terrible sound of a man's screams...

Andrew Haywood
Minster Photography
Micklegate
York

Dear Mr Holmes,

I searched my catalogue of images and found the enclosed. I trust it may serve your purpose? The young couple are most certainly Mr & Mrs Vandaleur. I have the collection paperwork to prove the fact (including Mr Vandaleur's signature). For my own part I knew them well enough as my sister's children attended the school they ran in Millington. If you wish I could forward on her details too, I know she would be only too happy to help. There are a good number of people in this area who would take no small pleasure in seeing that man brought to account.

Yours Sincerely,

Andrew Haywood

↑ *Letter from a relative of a child from Stapleton's old school.*

↑ *Photograph of Stapleton (aka Mr and Mrs Vandaleur).*

We heard the cry again, followed by the low, bass roar of the hound. Chasing through the night, we could only pray that we were in time to intervene between the beast and its prey. Another cry, this time brought short by a dull, heavy thud. Just ahead we perceived a crumpled figure in the moon light. Sir Henry's suit was immediately recognizable and it seemed all was lost. Holmes bent over the body before uttering a bizarre cry. "A beard!" he cried, "the man has a beard!" It would seem that the victim was not Sir Henry after all…

We identified the dead man as Selden, wearing clothes donated to him by Barrymore from Sir Henry's cast-offs. It was likely these clothes that had caused his death, Holmes noted, for certainly the mystery of Sir Henry's stolen boot could only be solved through one assumption: it had been taken to earn a tracking scent, hence the new, unworn boot had been returned and an old one taken in its place. Sir Henry's scent would have been all over his suit, of course, and the hound, when released by Stapleton to do its foul work, had found the wrong prey.

NOTTING HILL MURDERER'S BODY DISCOVERED ON THE MOOR

It is a great relief to those local to the moor that Selden, the Notting Hill Murderer, has at last been found and is most certainly beyond causing any further harm.

His body was discovered by two gentlemen walking the moor after the criminal had fallen from a rocky promontory and broken his neck. The death is being viewed as purely accidental, the result of the man losing his footing in territory that is infamous for its treacherous nature.

At that moment, we heard someone approach. Moving into the shadow of the rocks we observed Stapleton, no doubt checking on the success of his canine agent. Agreeing to silence on the subject of his guilt – in order for Holmes to buy the time he needed to gather proof – we revealed ourselves and promoted an assumption of accidental death. Holmes made it clear that his visit was brief and that he planned to return to London the following morning, washing his hands of a case that had yielded nothing in the way of facts. We could only hope our bluster convinced him, returning to Baskerville Hall and leaving Stapleton to the moor...

We took supper with Sir Henry – who was very much pleased to find Holmes now amongst us. My friend made a promise to the baronet that the affair was close to conclusion and that if he were to follow instructions to the letter matters would be favourably resolved soon enough. Holmes startled Sir Henry

Fear not, Cartwright, my presence is out in the open now but perhaps the situation is none the worse for it. Meet Dr. Watson and I at the train station in Coombe Tracey at 9.30 as I have one last mission for you!

The moment you arrive in London, I wish you to send a telegram, in my name, from Baker Street to Sir Henry telling him that if he finds the pocket-book which I have dropped he should return it to Baker Street by registered post (there is of course no such thing, the message is a simple ruse...)

Do that for me and, rest assured you shall know the outcome of all this on our return!

Holmes

and I by taking a great deal of interest in a portrait of Sir Hugo Baskerville – the black rogue who brought the troubled curse on his family all those years ago. He refused to comment on what had so captured his attention until Sir Henry had retired for the night, whereupon he led me back into the room, climbed up by the canvas and – using his arm to obscure the ringlets and hat – asked who I saw. The face of Stapleton sprung out of the canvas.

Holmes prepared the net that would see us catch Stapleton. He made it clear that Sir Henry should keep the dinner appointment he had arranged at Merripit House but warned him that he would do it alone. He should also send home his trap on arrival and make it clear that he intended to walk home. Sir Henry was beside himself at the notion but Holmes demanded the man's trust. That secured, Holmes wired Lestrade to come and join us and lay his final plans...

While we attended on the arrival of Lestrade, Holmes and I returned to Laura Lyons for a second interview. It was clear to Holmes that the lady had hopes of marrying Stapleton – who had presented himself as her potential lover – and it was his hope that by revealing Stapleton as a married man and liar, Mrs. Lyons might become a very useful ally.

Holmes showed Mrs. Lyons his proof as to Stapleton's deceit, her response was strong and immediate. "If he had kept faith with me I should have always done so with him," she admitted. The letter making the appointment with Sir Charles at the hour of his death had certainly been Stapleton's idea (in fact he had dictated the letter).

It was also his suggestion that she should not keep the appointment and deny knowledge of it after the fact so as not to throw suspicion on herself.

Once Lestrade had arrived we had time for a hasty dinner (with Holmes playing matters as close to his chest as usual) before we headed to Merripit House. We surrounded the place, being careful not to to disclose our presence to the inhabitants. Through the illuminated window of the cottage I could see Sir Henry and Stapleton but of Mrs. Stapleton there was no sign. A thick, white fog was making its way across the moor, causing Holmes great concern. "Our success," he commented, "and even Sir Henry's life may depend on upon his coming out before the fog is over the path."

My Dearest Laura,

It was, as always, the greatest pleasure to spend a few scant hours in your company today. Oh! For the day when we might always be together. That day is soon to come, my love, I am convinced of it. If only we could get the money you need to pay off that most perfidious husband, you could be divorced and then we could run to the very next church that would take us! It is a matter of the utmost dishonour to me that I have not the finances to effect your freedom, I will think of a way my love.

Always Yours,

X

↑ *Letter from Stapleton to Laura Lions.*

We drew back to higher ground and within a quarter of an hour we heard the sound of Sir Henry's quick footsteps on the path. But he was not alone... fresh on his heels could be discerned the continuous patter of something drawing towards us through the fog bank. Suddenly, it appeared. A hound it was, an enormous, coal-black hound, but not such a hound as mortal eyes have ever seen. Its eyes glowed, its muzzles and hackles were outlined in thickening flame. Never in the delirious dream of a disordered brain could anything more savage, more appalling, more hellish be conceived than that dark form that broke upon us out of the wall of fog.

HORROR HOUND TERRIFIES BARONET

Last night a horror story to rival the gothic imaginings within a penny dreadful played itself out in the moorland just outside Grimpen.

Our readers will certainly remember the tragic death of Sir Charles Baskerville in May of this year. No doubt many will also be familiar with the tales – often told yet scarcely believed – of the spectral hound that legend claims to haunt the area. It was that very hound – or an earthly approximation of it – that appeared within the fog of Grimpen Mire last night with its jaws intent on ending the life of yet another of the Baskerville family: Sir Henry Baskerville who has been resident in the family seat since the end of September. Thankfully the hound met its nemesis in the form of famed consulting detective, Sherlock Holmes. Having spent the last few weeks involving himself in the case, Mr Holmes lay a dangerous trap in order to capture both the beast and its murderous owner with no less a bait than the life of Sir Henry himself. Waiting on the moor in the company of his chronicler, Dr John Watson and Inspector Lestrade of Scotland Yard, Holmes leapt into action as the hound was set on the trail of Sir Henry, emptying five barrels of his pistol into the creature even as it set its fangs to the baronet's throat. Sir Henry is convalescing but is expected to make a full recovery.

The hound had been painted with a phosperous mixture to give it the flaming appearance of the legend and had been created by a Mr Stapleton of Merripit House. The name Stapleton was an alias disgusing the man's real identity: a former school-teacher called Vandaleur who fled the North of England with his wife after the deaths of three of the children in his care. While police possess more than enough evidence to imprison the man, his flight into the mire and subsequent disappearance suggest a future trial unlikely. It is widely believed that the villain met his end in the marshes and perhaps such a fate is more than fitting for his crimes. Mrs Vandaleur – who was presented as Stapleton's sister rather than wife – appears to have gone along with her husband's plans solely under the threat of violence. Mr Holmes has presented evidence that suggest she tried to warn Sir Henry of what was planned for him (including the posting of an anonymous note before he even arrived in the area) and that, plus the considerable signs of her physical abuse at her husband's hands, is expected to stand in her favour within the eyes of the law.

Further investigation – and the testimony of Mrs Vandaleur – has revealed that the hound was kept chained in an abandoned tin mine within Grimpen Mire until it was needed. The sounds of its distress have been heard frequently over the last months, perpetuating the legend of the Baskerville Hound even further.

Rodger Baskerville Jnr. (AKA Vandaleur, Stapleton)
Son of Rodger Baskerville who died in South America. Married Beryl Garcia and fled to England as 'Vandaleur'. Learning that he had two people between him and the Baskerville estate he moved to the area under a new pseudonym and set about plans to remove those that stood between him and his fortunes.

Upon hearing of the legendary hound from none other than Sir Charles Baskerville the seeds of his plan were sown...
(see Baskerville for full details).
Believed dead having vanished in Grimpen Mire.

THE FINAL PROBLEM

FRIDAY 24 APRIL TO MONDAY 4 MAY, 1891

FRENCH: HELP US SHERLOCK HOLMES

We have received word that the French government has hired famed consulting detective, Sherlock Holmes to assist them in a matter of "national importance". Details are sparse but it is believed that Mr. Holmes has been traveling the country incommunicado for the last couple of weeks and is expected to remain there some time. This is not the first time that Mr. Holmes has been employed in matters of such importance, his list of successes frequently ranging from the parochial to global. Nonetheless it is a matter of some considerable pride to see our nation turned to in the pursuit of the world's finest intellects and reasoners.

I had seen so little of Holmes that year, following his exploits through the press rather than – as had always been the case – in person. My life in practice and recent marriage took a priority over my time that left little room for other pursuits. It was with some surprise, therefore, that – on the evening of the 24th of April, 1891 – I found Holmes entering my consulting rooms looking very much the worse for wear. He apologized for his obvious ill-health and asked if I might object to his closing the shutters as he believed the rooms were under surveillance by a sniper. In another I would have taken such a statement as an obvious sign of delirium, but my friendship with Holmes was deep enough to lend his words the utmost seriousness. My faith was to be further tested by his request that I should join him on a trip to the Continent.

"Where?" I asked.

"Oh, anywhere," was his baffling reply.

Recognizing my confusion he began to explain: It was all to do with Professor Moriarty...

Watson,

You have perchance read of my engagement by the French government in a case of some interest. It is also an investigation of some delicacy so you will forgive me if I spare the details from a communication so ripe for intervention. It is an interesting and complex affair though the travel is considerable and I find myself yearning for the days when I could make these journeys through thought alone, fuelling the engine of my mind with data and tobacco. It cannot be helped, travel I must and I dare say there will be many more months of it before matters are resolved satisfactorily. We shall meet upon my return and it will be my singular pleasure to furnish you with the more interesting details in the matter.

Until then!

Holmes

Professor James Moriarty – (copied from Holmes' notes)

A man of good birth and excellent education, with a phenomenal mathematical faculty. At the age of twenty-one he wrote a treatise upon the Binomial Theorem, which has had a European vogue. On the strength of it he won the Mathematical Chair at one of our smaller universities, and had, to all appearances, a most brilliant career before him. But the man had hereditary tendencies of the most diabolical kind. A criminal strain ran in his blood, which, instead of being modified, was increased and rendered infinitely more dangerous by his extraordinary mental powers. Dark rumours gathered round him in the university town, and eventually he was compelled to resign his chair and to come down to London, where he set up as an army coach.

He is the Napoleon of crime, the organizer of half that is evil and nearly all that is undetected in London. He sits motionless, like a spider in the centre of its web, but that web has a thousand radiations, and he knows well every quiver of each of them. He does little himself. He only plans. But his agents are numerous and splendidly organized. Is there a crime to be done, a paper to be abstracted, we will say, a house to be rifled, a man to be removed – the word is passed to the Professor, the matter is organized and carried out. The agent may be caught. In that case money is found for his bail or his defence. But the central power which uses the agent is never caught – never so much as suspected.

Patterson,

He is on to us. I have, just this minute, received a visit from our friend, Moriarty.

He is extremely tall and thin, his forehead domes out in a white curve, and his two eyes are deeply sunken in this head. He is clean-shaven, pale, and ascetic-looking, retaining something of the professor in his features. His shoulders are rounded from much study, and his face protrudes forward, and is forever slowly oscillating from side to side in a curiously reptilian fashion.

He means to end my life - for you and I know that there lies no other recourse to escape for the man - and the visit held the sole purpose of "warning me off" our case.

"You crossed my patch on the 4th of January," said he. "On the 23d you incommoded me; by the middle of February I was seriously inconvenienced by you; at the end of March I was absolutely hampered in my plans; and now, at the close of April, I find myself placed in such a position through your continual persecution that I am in positive danger of losing my liberty. The situation is becoming an impossible one."

His solution was predictable: I must drop the matter. You know me well enough to intuit my reply.

It is clear I must now go to ground. Matters cannot be resolved until Monday and if I hope to retain my life I must somehow avoid the reach of his agents. You will understand if I do not set down my intentions here but I can assure you that I will keep in touch and ask only that you keep your resolve in this matter as surely as I will keep mine.

Holmes

We marked our suitcases for Paris and then left them to their journey (in the hope they might confuse any pursuers), travelling from Newhaven to Dieppe, then heading into Switzerland via Luxembourg and Basle.

221 BAKER St. ABLAZE!

The rooms of Mr. Sherlock Holmes caught fire last night. Details are hard to come by though it is believed that nobody was harmed in the conflaguration. Inspector Patterson, the investigating officer, refused to be drawn on the notion that the fire might be an act of arson against the famed detective insisting that there was little evidence to point to such a conclusion. It must be said though that it is difficult to imagine a man in London with more enemies amongst the criminal fraternity.

Internationalen Telegramm

SW654 LD9732	International Wire	Preis 3chf	Urgent!

Von
Sherlock Holmes
Strasbourg, France April 27th

Adresse
Inspector Patterson
Scotland Yard, London

What news?

PM JAN24

gesendet von Hans Densieren

Dieses Telegramm wird akzeptiert, die den Regeln und Vorschriften der Schweizer System-Telegramm. Bekanntmachung über die diese Regeln sind auf der Rückseite dieses Formulars. Fehler werden immer noch für eine technische, es sei denn, der Natur.

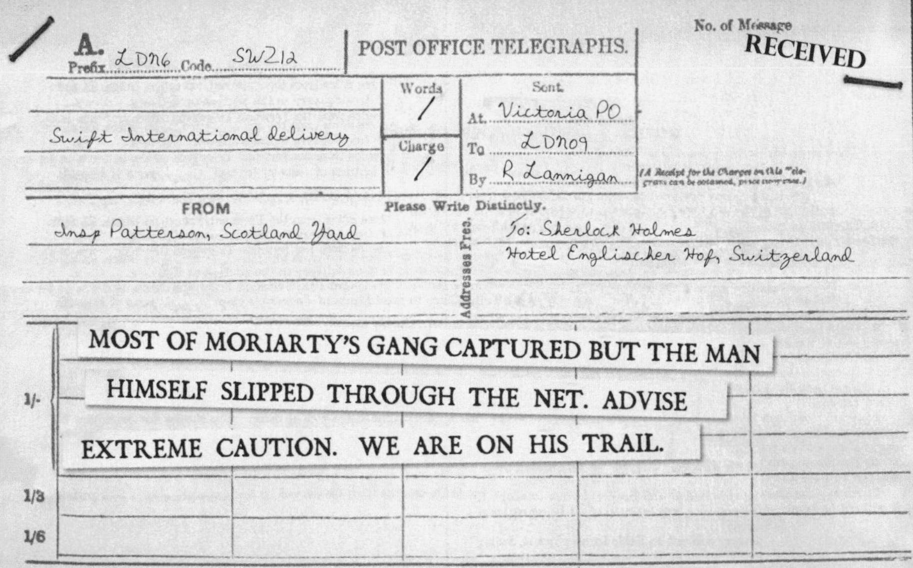

A. Prefix LDN6 Code SW212

POST OFFICE TELEGRAPHS.

No. of Message

RECEIVED

Swift International delivery

Words 1

Charge 1

Sent.
At Victoria PO
To LDN09
By R Lannigan

(A Receipt for the Charges on this Telegram can be obtained, price one penny.)

FROM
Insp Patterson, Scotland Yard

Please Write Distinctly.

Addresses Free.

To: Sherlock Holmes
Hotel Englischer Hof, Switzerland

1/-

MOST OF MORIARTY'S GANG CAPTURED BUT THE MAN HIMSELF SLIPPED THROUGH THE NET. ADVISE EXTREME CAUTION. WE ARE ON HIS TRAIL.

1/3

1/6

NOTICE TO THE SENDER ~~OF THIS TELEGRAM.~~
This Telegram will be accepted for transmission subject to the Regulations made pursuant to the 15th Section of the Telegraph Act, 1868, and to the Notice printed at the back hereof.

(HARRISON & SONS. PRINTERS, LONDON)

Englischer Hof
Meiringen, Switzerland

Herr Watson,

Not long after your departure an English lady in the final stages of consumption arrived at my door in great distress. She had wintered in Davos Platz and was journeying to join her friends at Lucerne when the haemorrage overtook her. It seems that there is little that can be done to aid her but it would unquestionably be of some comfort were you, an English Doctor, to attend to her in her final hours. I hesitate to ask but find I am at a loss as to an alternative, could you return at your earliest opportunity?

Your Servant,

Peter Steiler

ps. I view your compliance as a considerable favour since the lady will not see a Swiss physician and I cannot but feel that I am incurring a great responsibility. I will be much in your debt.

My Dear Watson
I write these few lines through the courtesy of Mr Moriarty, who awaits my convenience for the final discussion of those questions which lie between us. He has been giving me a sketch of the methods by which he avoided the English police and kept himself informed of our movements. They certainly confirm the very high opinion which I had formed of his abilities. I am pleased to think that I shall be able to free society from any further effects of his presence, though I fear that it is at a cost which will give pain to my friends, and especially, my dear Watson, to you. I have already explained to you, however, that my career had in any case reached its crisis, and that no possible conclusion to it could be more congenial to me than this. Indeed, if I may make a full confession to you, I was quite convinced that the letter from Meiringen was a hoax, and I allowed you to depart on that errand under the persuasion that some development of this sort would follow. Tell Inspector Patterson that the papers which he needs to convict the gang are in pigeonhole M.,

done up in a blue envelope and inscribed "Moriarty." I made every disposition of property before leaving England and handed it to my brother Mycroft. Pray give my greetings to Mrs Watson, and believe me to be, my dear fellow

Very sincerely yours,

Sherlock Holmes

FAMED DETECTIVE MISSING, BELIEVED DEAD

(Via Reuters) Consulting detective, Sherlock Holmes is believed to have died last night, plunging into the waters of the Reichenbach Falls in Switzerland. The English police force – who have worked in conjunction with Holmes on innumerate occasions – are pursuing an assumption of foul play in the detective's death. Holmes' life had been threatened several times in connection with a current investigation and it is regretfully assumed that the repeated attempts to silence him were finally successful.

After a lengthy period working alongside the French government Mr. Holmes is believed to have been holidaying with his long-time friend, Dr John Watson. Dr Watson has long been Holmes' chronicler as well as friend, detailing a number of the detective's cases for the readers of London's *Strand Magazine*. No doubt the final matters of this most august of criminal reasoners will be fully elaborated upon in due course within those very pages. Until then we are forced to piece together the details as the facts allow.

According to the proprietor of the Englischer Hof, Peter Steiner the elder, he had suggested his guests visit the Falls that morning. An hour or so after Holmes and Watson had left for the mountains another English gentleman arrived enquiring after a room and asking to borrow a sheet of the hotel stationery. Herr Steiner gladly obliged and thought no more upon the matter until Dr Watson returned some time later bearing a letter written on the hotel paper (and falsely signed in Steiner's name) asking the doctor to attend as a matter of urgency, there being a sick lady at the guesthouse in need of medical attention.

It is clear in hindsight that this was nothing more than a ruse to remove Dr. Watson from his colleague's side. Certainly, by the time Dr. Watson returned to the falls there was no sign of Holmes. The mysterious Englishman has been described as "aged and pale" but there are no other clues as to his identity at the present time.

Times

Dear Sir,

I have stood by and allowed the good reputation of my brother to be continually sullied in the gossip columns of this town's "papers". No longer. I am sickened by the relentless tittle-tattle surrounding my late and much lamented brother Professor James Moriarty. During the last few months of his life he was pursued and victimized by that most questionable of national "heroes" Mr. Sherlock Holmes. His every moment made a misery by the continuing accusations and interference of this "consulting detective".

My brother was a much lauded mathematician, a logician and researcher. He was a man who brought a great deal of worth to the world's intellectual landscape. Certainly his achievements in the field of physics and astronomy were a greater contribution to refined society than the penny dreadful exploits of Holmes (that I suspect are closer to works of fiction than the fact their author claims them to be). Why then must I sit quietly as his name is besmirched in connection with the death of this petty amateur? I am quite sure that my brother and Holmes fell together on that fateful day, I am quite sure also that it was the final act of an egocentric lunatic that took my brother from me. Holmes is a murderer, of that I have no doubt and if there is any justice left in this country we will see his posthumous reputation in tatters for it.

Yours Faithfully
James Moriarty (Col.)

THE ADVENTURE OF THE EMPTY HOUSE

SATURDAY, 31 MARCH TO THURSDAY, 5 APRIL 1894

↑ *My wife, too, had sadly died, and I visited her grave every Sunday.*

At the commencement of this case I was sure of only one thing: Sherlock Holmes was dead.

It can be imagined that my close intimacy with Sherlock Holmes had interested me deeply in crime, and that after his disappearance I never failed to read with care the various problems which came before the public.

There was none, however, which appealed to me like the tragedy of Ronald Adair. As I read the evidence at the inquest, which led to a verdict of wilful murder against some person or persons unknown, I realized more clearly than I had ever done the loss that the community had sustained by the death of Sherlock Holmes.

There were points about this strange business which would, I was sure, have especially appealed to him, and the efforts of the police would have been supplemented, or more probably anticipated, by the trained observation and the alert mind of the first criminal agent in Europe.

METROPOLITAN POLICE

31 March 1894

Scotland Yard **Station** Colonel Sebastian Moran **WITNESS**

My last contact with Mr Adair was when we played a rubber of whist at the Bagatelle club. Mr Murray and Sir John Hardy were also there. It was a fair game, equally spread around, and Ronald lost only about five pounds, not much to him as ... he was fairly well off. Wasn't his first game, either: he's been doing the rounds of the clubs, usually winning out. He even won about four hundred and twenty pounds in a sitting a few weeks ago from Godfrey Milner and Lord Balmoral. Afterwards he left, said he was heading home; that was at about 9.30 in the evening.

↗ *Adair often played whist at various clubs, according to witness reports I obtained from "friends" at Scotland Yard.*

31 March 1894

METROPOLITAN POLICE

Scotland Yard **STATION** Emilia Sayers **WITNESS**

I heard him come into the front room on the second floor; it's used as a sitting room. I'd lit a fire, but it got too smoky so I had to open a window, and then left him to it. Didn't hear nothing until 11.20, that's when Lady Maynooth and her daughter got back. They wanted to say goodnight and she tried to get into his room. But the door was locked on the inside and crying and knocking didn't do anything. Me and the gentleman's valet had to help them shove the door open and then he was just lying on the floor near the table, his head all ... burst, I couldn't look for long. They said it was an expanding bullet that done it. There was a lot of money on the table and some paper, it looked like he was figuring out how much he'd won or lost.

↗ *This calibre of bullet was used for Adair's assassination in Park Lane.*

I made my way to Park Lane to investigate. As I did so, I struck against an elderly deformed man, who had been behind me, and I knocked down several books that he was carrying. Naturally, I helped to pick them up, and gave them to him, but with a snarl of contempt he turned upon his heel. I observed the window of the house and found it was, truly, inaccessible, and then returned to my house. I had not been in my study five minutes when the maid entered to say that a person desired to see me. To my astonishment, it was none other than my strange old book-collector. "You're surprised to see me, sir," said he, in a strange, croaking voice. Indeed I was.

Further Notes on the Case

- *No reason why the young man should have fastened the door upon the inside.*
- *Drop from window very high, no marks in flower bed or on path.*
- *Park Lane a frequented thoroughfare, cab stand within a hundred yards of the house. No one had heard shot.*
- *Revolver bullet mushroomed out, as soft-nosed bullets will, causing instant death.*

↑ *Holmes said both he and Moriarty had underestimated each other's strength.*

"Well, sir, I thought I'd just step in and tell you that if I was a bit gruff in my manner, I am much obliged to you for picking up my books. I am a neighbour of yours. You'll find my little bookshop at the corner of Church Street. With five volumes you could just fill that gap on that second shelf. It looks untidy, does it not, sir?"

I moved my head to look at the cabinet behind me. When I turned again, Sherlock Holmes was standing smiling at me across my study table.

I must have fainted for the first and last time in my life. Certainly a grey mist swirled before my eyes, and when it cleared I found Holmes sitting by my side.

"My dear Watson, I owe you a thousand apologies. I had no idea that you would be so affected."

"Holmes!" I cried. "Is it really you? Good heavens, to think that you – you of all men – should be standing in my study! I am overjoyed to see you! Tell me how you came alive out of that dreadful chasm."

"I never was in it. I perceived the somewhat sinister figure of the late Professor Moriarty standing upon the narrow pathway which led to safety. He drew no weapon, but he rushed at me and threw his long arms around me!

"We tottered together upon the brink of the fall. I have some knowledge, however, of baritsu, the Japanese system of wrestling which has more than once been very useful to me. I slipped through his grip, and he with a horrible scream kicked madly for a few seconds, clawed the air with both his hands, and over he went. I saw him fall for a long way. Then he struck a rock, bounced off, and splashed into the water."

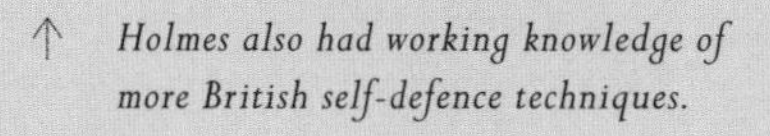

↑ *Holmes also had working knowledge of more British self-defence techniques.*

A small sketch made by Holmes in Italy. →

← *Reports had appeared in the newspaper of Holmes' alias, Norwegian explorer Sigerson.*

BARRINGTON POLAR TEAM RETURN SAFE

CAPTAIN JAMES BARRINGTON and his entire team of explorers thankfully returned to London at 8 p.m. yesterday evening, safe and relatively unharmed. The men of the group were in good spirits, and Captain Barrington was particularly insistent that their unsuccessful attempt for the South Pole may have resulted in all their deaths, had it not been for the assistance of famed Norwegian adventurer Sigerson, who had been passing through the area and provided "both physical and spiritual" assistance. Barrington described Sigerson as a "stoic fellow not much given to conversation but with a steely core almost like that of an Englishman". The men confirmed they would spend time with their families before planning another attempt next year.

Holmes recounted how he had scaled the sheer face of the cliff, and had been lying on a ledge in exhaustion when my group had investigated the scene and left. Then he had been attacked with rocks, and concluded that the Professor had a confederate who had witnessed his death and was attempting to complete the task of causing Holmes' own. Only by scrambling down to the path and running into the forest did he evade death, and a week later found himself in Florence.

"I owe you many apologies, my dear Watson, but it was all-important that it should be thought I was dead, and it is quite certain that you would not have written so convincing an account of my unhappy end had you not yourself thought that it was true.

"As to Mycroft, I had to confide in him in order to obtain the money which I needed. The course of events in London left two of the Moriarty gang's most dangerous members at liberty. I travelled for two years in Tibet, visiting Lhasa and spending some days with the head Lama. You may have read of the remarkable explorations of a Norwegian named Sigerson, but I am sure that it never occurred to you that you were receiving news of your friend. I then passed through Persia, looked in at Mecca, and paid a short but interesting visit to the Khalifa at Khartoum. Returning to France, I spent some months in a research into the coal-tar derivatives, which I conducted in a laboratory at Montpelier, in the South of France.

"We have three years of the past to discuss. Let that suffice until half-past nine, when we start upon the notable adventure of the empty house."

Holmes led me out into a cab. I imagined that we were bound for Baker Street, but he stopped the cab at the corner of Cavendish Square.

At every subsequent street corner he took the utmost pains to assure that he was not followed. We passed rapidly through a network of mews and stables. I attempted to note it down as a precaution against having to retrace our steps, but was outfoxed by Holmes' rapid and assured step, and gave up.

We emerged into Blandford Street, passed through a wooden gate into a deserted yard, and then opened with a key the back door of a house. We entered and he closed it behind us.

The place was pitch-dark, but it was evident that it was an empty house. Our feet creaked and crackled over the bare planking, and my outstretched hand touched a wall from which the paper was hanging in ribbons. Holmes turned suddenly to the right, and we found ourselves in a large, square, empty room, heavily shadowed in the corners, but faintly lit in the centre by the lights of the street beyond.

"Do you know where we are?" he whispered.

"Surely that is Baker Street," I answered.

"Exactly. We are in Camden House, which stands opposite to our own old quarters."

"But why are we here?"

"Because it commands so excellent a view of that picturesque pile. Draw a little nearer to the window and then to look up at our old rooms – the starting-point of so many of our little adventures!"

I crept forward and looked across at the familiar window. As my eyes fell upon it I gave a gasp and a cry of amazement. The blind was down and a strong light was burning in the room. The shadow of a man who was seated in a chair within was thrown in hard, black outline, like one of those silhouettes that our grandparents loved to frame. It was a perfect reproduction of Holmes! So amazed was I that I threw out my hand to make sure that the man himself was standing beside me.

Sometimes I felt the bust displayed more emotion than Holmes himself! Its maker declined to charge for the honour of its creation. →

- *Left onto Margaret Street*
- *Right onto Great Portland Street*
- *Through Mews Market Place*
- *Leave Mews Market Place*
- *Left onto Great Titchfield street*
- *Left into barn at Margaret St (again?)*
- *From barn to annex off Regent St(?)*
- *Left into alley nr ~~Great~~ Little Portland Street*
- *Right into stables in ???*
- *Right???*

Buste du torse – no charge
por le honneur de
M. Oscar Meunier
14, Rue St Nicolas, Grenoble

"It really is rather like me, is it not?"

"I should be prepared to swear that it was you."

"The credit of the execution is due to Monsieur Oscar Meunier, of Grenoble, who spent some days in doing the moulding. It is a bust in wax. The rest I arranged myself during my visit to Baker Street this afternoon.

"I had the strongest possible reason for wishing certain people to think that I was there when I was really elsewhere."

"And the rooms are watched?"

"By the charming society whose leader lies in the Reichenbach Fall. You must remember that only they knew that I was still alive. They watched them continuously, and this morning they saw me arrive.

"I recognized their sentinel when I glanced out of my window."

"I cared nothing for him. But I cared a great deal for the much more formidable person who was behind him, the bosom friend of Moriarty, the man who dropped the rocks over the cliff, the most cunning and dangerous criminal in London. That is the man who is after me tonight, Watson, and that is the man who is quite unaware that we are after him."

Parker
Harmless
Garroter (part-retired)
Remarkable performer on Jew's harp

According to Holmes' notes, the sentinel Parker was not significant. ↑

Mrs Hudson,

Kindly make one of the following changes every quarter hour, randomly selected for realism:

- Looking out window
- Examining bookcase
- By chemistry equipment
- Unseen by window
- Seated in chair
- "Speaking" towards parlour
- Addressing you

We waited in silence for what felt like hours. I clutched Holmes' arm and pointed upwards.

"The shadow has moved!" I cried.

"Am I such a farcical bungler, Watson, that I should erect an obvious dummy and expect that some of the sharpest men in Europe would be deceived by it? Mrs Hudson has made some change in that figure eight times."

A low, stealthy sound came to my ears from the back of the house in which we lay concealed. A door opened and shut. An instant later, steps crept down the passage, reverberating through the house. Holmes and I crouched back against the wall, my hand closing upon the handle of my revolver.

Peering through the gloom, I saw the outline of a man. He was within three yards of us before I realised that he had no idea of our presence. He passed close beside us, stole over to the window, and raised it. He was an elderly man, with a thin, projecting nose, a high, bald forehead and a huge grizzled moustache.

Then from the pocket of his overcoat he drew a bulky object. He bent forward and threw all his weight and strength upon some lever, with a long, grinding noise and a powerful click. I saw that he held in his hand a sort of gun, with a curiously misshapen butt. He rested the end of the barrel upon the ledge of the open window, and I saw his long moustache droop over the stock and his eye gleam as it peered along the sights. Then his finger tightened on the trigger. There was a strange, loud whizz and a long, silvery tinkle of broken glass. At that instant Holmes sprang like a tiger on to the marksman's back and hurled him flat upon his face. I fell upon him, and my comrade blew a shrill call upon a whistle. There was the clatter of running feet and two policemen with one plain-clothes detective rushed into the room.

"That you, Lestrade?" said Holmes.

"Yes, Mr Holmes. I took the job myself. It's good to see you back in London, sir."

Lestrade had produced two candles and I was able at last to have a good look at our prisoner.

"You fiend!" he kept on muttering. "You clever, clever fiend!"

"I have not introduced you yet," said Holmes. This, gentlemen, is Colonel Sebastian Moran, once of Her Majesty's Indian Army, and the best heavy game shot that our Eastern Empire has ever produced."

Holmes had picked up the air gun from the floor and was examining its mechanism.

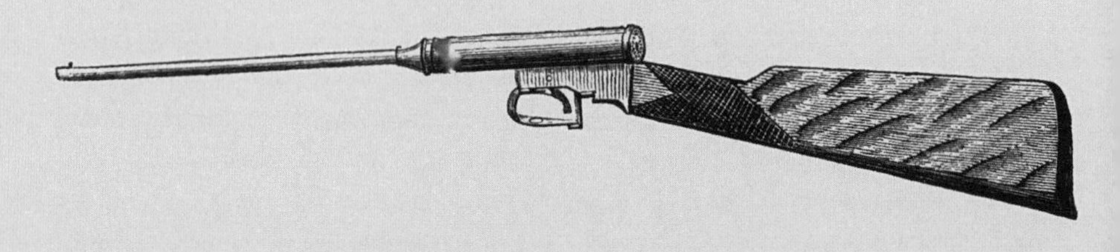

↑ *The ingenious weapon is on display in the Black Museum, I believe.*

↑ *Moran was deceptively strong but seemed to recognize his defeat.*

"An admirable and unique weapon," said he, "noiseless and of tremendous power. I knew Von Herder, the blind German mechanic who constructed it to the order of the late Professor Moriarty. A soft revolver bullet, Watson. There's genius in that, for who would expect to find such a thing fired from an air gun?"

"You have not made it clear what was Colonel Moran's motive in murdering the Honourable Ronald Adair."

"Colonel Moran and young Adair had between them won a considerable amount of money. On the day of the murder Adair had discovered that Moran was cheating and had threatened to expose him unless he voluntarily resigned his membership. The exclusion from his clubs would mean ruin to Moran, who lived by his ill-gotten card gains. He murdered Adair.

"Colonel Moran will trouble us no more, the famous air gun of Von Herder will embellish the Scotland Yard Museum, and once again I am free to examine those interesting little problems which the complex life of London presents."

↓ *Past glory is no guarantee of honesty. I'll admit I can't see where this card is marked.*

Current record of most tigers bagged by club members

Col. Sebastian Moran – 51
Count Leopold Veronsky – 12
Col. Arbuthnot Prendergast (Retired) – 4
Sir Rodney Haversham-White – 1 and a half

Recorded by club secretary William Bailey.

NO. 8

OFFICIAL REPORT

REFERENCE TO PAPERS:

METROPOLITAN POLICE

Scotland Yard STATION Insp. Lestrade

NAME: Moran, Sebastian, Colonel.
(Possible alias Count Negretto Sylvius)

EMPLOYMENT: Unemployed.
Formerly 1st Bangalore Pioneers.

BORN: London, 1840. Son of Sir Augustus Moran, C.B., once British Minister to Persia.

EDUCATION: Eton and Oxford.

Served in Jowaki Campaign, Afghan Campaign, Charasiab (despatches), Sherpur, and Cabul.

ADDRESS: Conduit Street.

CLUBS: The Anglo-Indian, the Tankerville, the Bagatelle Card Club.

Confirmed crimes: Attempted murder of Mr Sherlock Holmes at Reichenbach Falls with rocks, boulders

Murder of Honorable Ronald Adair

Alleged/Unconfirmed Crimes: Number of criminal assassinations, blackmail, burglary and trespassing, forgery.

↑ *A Scotland Yard report on Sebastian Moran, a known criminal and cohort of Professor Moriarty.*

THE ADVENTURE OF THE NORWOOD BUILDER

TUESDAY, 21 AUGUST 1894

Mr Sherlock Holmes was unfolding his morning paper in a leisurely fashion when our attention was arrested by a tremendous ring at the bell, followed immediately by a hollow drumming sound, as if someone were beating on the outer door with his fist. Rapid feet clattered up the stair and a wild-eyed young man burst into the room.

"I'm sorry, Mr Holmes," he cried. "You mustn't blame me. I am the unhappy John Hector McFarlane."

"You mention your name as if I should recognize it, but I assure you that, beyond the obvious facts that you are a bachelor, a solicitor, a Freemason and an asthmatic, I know nothing whatever about you."

↑ *McFarlane entered the room out of breath and wild eyed.*

John Hector McFarlane
JUNIOR PARTNER

GRAHAM AND MCFARLANE
426, Gresham Buildings, E.C.

↑ *Deepdene House, residence of Jonas Oldacre.*

Our client stared in amazement. "If they come to arrest me, make them give me time so that I may tell you the whole truth!"

"On what charge do you expect to be arrested?"

"Upon the charge of murdering Mr Jonas Oldacre, of Lower Norwood."

Our visitor stretched forward a quivering hand and picked up The Daily Telegraph, *which still lay upon Holmes' knee. He indicated the relevant page, and I read the story aloud as Mr Holmes made notes. Holmes sat forward. "May I ask how it is that you are still at liberty, since there*

The incriminating cane that McFarlane had left behind.

appears to be enough evidence to justify your arrest?"

"I live at Torrington Lodge, Blackheath, with my parents, but last night, having to do business very late with Mr Oldacre, I stayed at an hotel in Norwood, and came to my business from there. I knew nothing of this affair until I was in the train! I at once saw the horrible danger of my position, and I hurried to put the case into your hands."

A moment later Lestrade appeared in the doorway. "One moment, Lestrade," said Holmes. "This gentleman was about to give us an account of this affair, which might aid us in clearing it up."

Lestrade considered this grimly. "I'll give you half an hour," said he.

McFarlane related his tale. Oldacre was familiar to him as being known by his parents, but he was surprised when at three o'clock he entered his office and bade him cast his will into "proper legal shape" from a notebook sheet of scribbled writing. McFarlane realized with astonishment the old man intended to leave everything to him! Oldacre claimed he had no living relations and, knowing McFarlane's parents, felt him to be a deserving young man. The older man informed him there were a number of other documents that he should see, thus he would be obliged if he would visit him at his house for supper at nine. McFarlane did as he was bid, being admitted by a middle-aged housekeeper, and worked with Oldacre until 11.30, when he was instructed to leave via the French windows so as not to wake the housekeeper.

Holmes asked to see the will notes in question. "This was written in a train; the good writing represents stations, the bad writing movement, and the very bad writing passing over points! It is curious that a man should draw up so important a document in so haphazard a fashion."

Oldacre: Builder, bachelor, practically a hermit, age 52
- Deepdene House: Small timber yard at back of house
- Fire in yard reported at 12, fire brigade, then inquiry
- House examined, found empty, bed not slept in Safe open, papers scattered

- Signs of a struggle, slight traces of blood, walking stick slightly stained, property of McFarlane
- French windows open, drag-marks to woodpile
- Charred remains found in woodpile
- **Lestrade investigating**

→ *McFarlane's note shows he and Oldacre had a lot of business to get through.*

Oldacre Papers
- Will
- Building Leases (5)
- Title Deeds (3)
- Various Scrip
- An "IOU"
- Miscellaneous

This is the last will and testement of me
Jonas Oldacre of Lower Norwood in the London
Borrough of Lambeth made this twentieth day
of August in the year of our Lord one thousand
eight hundred and ninty four.

I give and bequeeth unto Mr John Hector
McFarlane all my real and personal estates money
household objects and all other property from
whatever source it may arise for him during his
life after which at his decease the property he
dies possessed of to be disposed however he
sees fit in his own will.

I do also appoint the aformentioned John Hector
McFarlane of Graham McFarlane trustee to this
my said will In witness whereof I the said Jonas
Oldacre the testater have to this my last will and
testement set my hand and seal the day and year
first above written.

↑ *The hastily scribbled, handwritten will of Jonas Oldacre of Deep Dene House, Sydenham.*

→ *A clipping from the* Daily Telegraph *containing an article about the suspicious disappearance of Jonas Oldacre.*

Daily Teleg

21 August, 1894

MYSTERIOUS AFFAIR AT LOWER NORWOOD.

DISAPPEARANCE OF A WELL-KNOWN BUILDER. SUSPICION OF MURDER AND ARSON. A CLUE TO THE CRIMINAL

Late last night, or early this morning, an incident occurred at Lower Norwood which points, it is feared, to a serious crime. Mr Jonas Oldacre is a well-known resident of that suburb, where he has carried on his business as a builder for many years. Mr Oldacre is a bachelor, fifty-two years of age, and lives in Deep Dene House, at the Sydenham end of the road of that name. He has had the reputation of being a man of eccentric habits, secretive and retiring. For some years he has practically withdrawn from the business, in which he is said to have amassed considerable wealth. A small timber-yard still exists, however, at the back of the house, and last night, about twelve o'clock, an alarm was given that one of the stacks was on fire. The engines were soon upon the spot, but the dry wood burned with great fury, and it was impossible to arrest the conflagration until the stack had been entirely consumed. Up to this point the incident bore the appearance of an ordinary accident, but fresh indications seem to point to serious crime. Surprise was expressed at the absence of the master of the establishment from the scene of the fire, and an inquiry followed, which showed that he had disappeared from the house. An examination of his room revealed that the bed had not been slept in, that a safe which stood in it was open, that a number of important papers were scattered about the room, and, finally, that there were signs of a murderous struggle, slight traces of blood being found within the room, and an oaken walking-stick, which also showed stains of blood upon the handle. It is known that Mr Jonas Oldacre had received a late visitor in his bedroom upon that night, and the stick found has been identified as the property of this person, who is a young London solicitor named John Hector McFarlane, junior partner of Graham and McFarlane, of 426, Gresham Buildings, E.C. The police believe that they have evidence in their possession which supplies a very convincing motive for the crime, and altogether it cannot be doubted that sensational developments will follow.

Later. -- It is rumoured as we go to press that Mr John Hector McFarlane has actually been arrested on the charge of the murder of Mr Jonas Oldacre. It is at least certain that a warrant has been issued. There have been further and sinister developments in the investigation at Norwood. Besides the signs of a struggle in the room of the unfortunate builder it is now known that the French windows of his bedroom (which is on the ground floor) were found to be open, that there were marks as if some bulky object had been dragged across to the wood-pile, and, finally, it is asserted that charred remains have been found among the charcoal ashes of the fire. The police theory is that a most sensational crime has been committed, that the victim was clubbed to death in his own bedroom, his papers rifled, and his dead body dragged across to the wood-stack, which was then ignited so as to hide all traces of the crime. The conduct of the criminal investigation has been left in the experienced hands of Inspector Lestrade, of Scotland Yard, who is following up the clues with his accustomed energy and sagacity.

Tragic Discovery

Holmes rose and made his preparations for the day's work.

"My first movement must be in the direction of Blackheath. It is evident to me that the logical way to approach the case is to begin by trying to throw some light upon the first incident – the curious will, so suddenly made, and to so unexpected an heir!"

It was late when my friend returned. His detailed notes revealed the extent to which his high hopes were unfulfilled.

↑ *McFarlane's ticket to Blackheath.*

I went there, and I found very quickly that Oldacre was a pretty considerable blackguard. McFarlane's mother was at home - a little, fluffy, blue-eyed person, in a tremor of fear and indignation.

"He was more like a malignant and cunning ape than a human being," said she, "and he always was, ever since he was a young man. In fact, he was an old suitor of mine. Thank Heaven that I had the sense to turn away from him. I was engaged to him, Mr Holmes, when I heard a shocking story of how he had turned a cat loose in an aviary, and I was so horrified at his brutal cruelty that I would have nothing more to do with him."

She rummaged and produced a photograph of a woman, shamefully defaced and mutilated with a knife. "That is my own photograph," she said. "He sent it to me in that state, with his curse, upon my wedding morning."

← *The photograph, mutilated with vicious malice.*

Well, after that I tried one or two leads, but I gave it up at last and off I went to Norwood. This place, Deepdene House, is a big modern villa of staring brick, standing back in its own grounds, with a laurel-clumped lawn in front of it. Here is a rough plan:

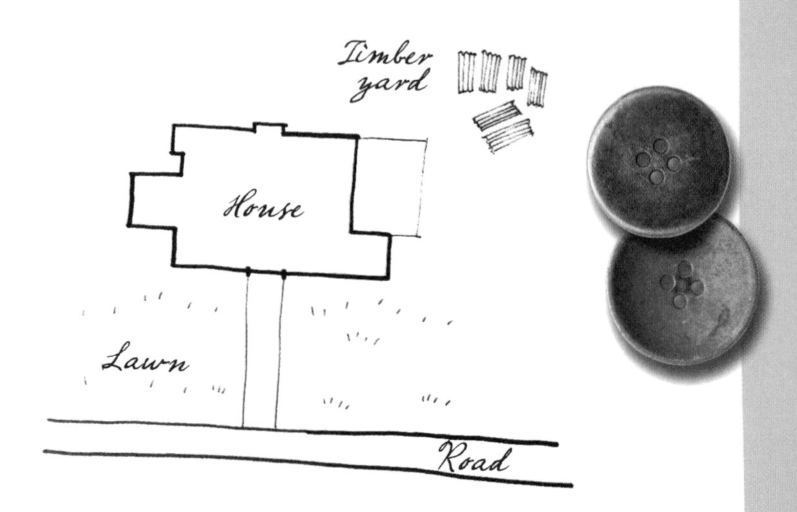

Lestrade was not there, but his head constable did the honours. They had spent the morning raking among the ashes of the burned woodpile, and besides the charred organic remains they had secured several discoloured metal discs. I examined them with care, and there was no doubt that they were trouser buttons. I even distinguished that one of them was marked with the name of 'Hyams', who was Oldacre's tailor. I went into the bedroom and examined that also. The bloodstains were very slight, mere smears and discolourations, but undoubtedly fresh. The stick had been removed, but there also the marks were slight. There is no doubt about the stick belonging to our client. He admits it.

Only one little gleam of hope did I get - and yet it amounted to nothing. I examined the contents of the safe, most of which had been taken out and left on the table. The papers had been made up into sealed envelopes, one or two of which had been opened by the police.

It seemed to me that all the papers were not there. This, of course, would turn Lestrade's argument against himself, for who would steal a thing if he knew that he would shortly inherit it?

I tried my luck with the housekeeper. Mrs Lexington is her name, a little, dark, silent person, with suspicious and sidelong eyes. She knew nothing of the papers, nor of Mr Oldacre's private affairs.

So, my dear Watson, there's my report of a failure.

Holmes bristled. "Unless we succeed in establishing an alternative theory, this man is lost. One curious point: on looking over the bank book I found that the low state of the balance was principally due to large cheques which have been made out during the last year to a Mr Cornelius."

The next morning I came down to breakfast to find Holmes holding an open telegram. "What do you think of this, Watson?"

"It is Lestrade's little cock-a-doodle of victory," he continued with a bitter smile.

Holmes left his untouched meal behind him and started with me for Norwood. Lestrade greeted us with a triumphant grin. "Step this way and I think I can convince you that it was John McFarlane who carried out this crime."

He led us through the passage and struck a match to show a bloodstained thumbprint on the wall. He then produced a wax impression of McFarlane's thumb, and showed how the two were identical. It was evident to me that our client was lost. And yet Sherlock Holmes was visibly writhing with inward merriment!

"What a providential thing that this young man should press his right thumb against the wall in taking his hat from the peg! But why didn't the police see this mark yesterday?"

"My dear Lestrade," said Holmes, his two eyes shining like stars, "there is an important witness whom you have not seen."

Reluctantly, at Holmes's prompting, we took some straw from the yard to the top

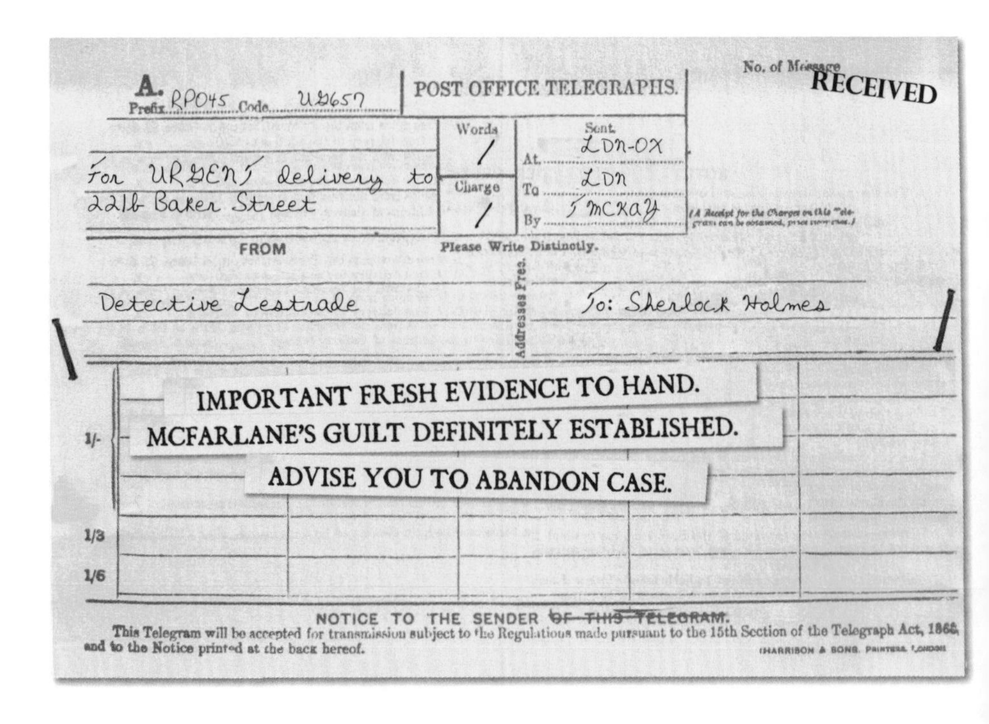
A. Prefix RPO45 Code U2657

POST OFFICE TELEGRAPHS.

No. of Message

RECEIVED

Words 1

Charge 1

Sent At LDN-OX To LDN By J McKAY

For URGENT delivery to 221b Baker Street

FROM

Please Write Distinctly.

Addresses Free.

Detective Lestrade

To: Sherlock Holmes

1/-

IMPORTANT FRESH EVIDENCE TO HAND.
MCFARLANE'S GUILT DEFINITELY ESTABLISHED.
ADVISE YOU TO ABANDON CASE.

1/3

1/6

NOTICE TO THE SENDER ~~OF THIS TELEGRAM.~~

This Telegram will be accepted for transmission subject to the Regulations made pursuant to the 15th Section of the Telegraph Act, 1868, and to the Notice printed at the back hereof.

(HARRISON & SONS, PRINTERS, LONDON)

No, A^A35772 London 23rd March 1892
The Union Bank of London Limited
HOLBORN CIRCUS BRANCH
Pay Mr Cornelius or Order
Twenty guineas
20.00
J. Oldacre
UNION BANK OF LONDON LIMITED
This Cheque must be endorsed by the party to whom it is payable.

← *Lestrade and the other policemen present were amazed.*

corridor. With buckets of water at the ready, we put a match to it and shouted, "Fire!"

A door suddenly flew open out of what appeared to be solid wall at the end of the corridor, and a little, wizened man darted out of it, like a rabbit from its burrow.

"Capital!" said Holmes, calmly. "Lestrade, allow me to present you with your principal missing witness… Mr Jonas Oldacre."

Oldacre gave an uneasy laugh, shrinking back from the furious red face of the angry detective. "I have done no harm."

"There's the advantage of being a builder," said Holmes. "He was able to fix up his own little hiding-place without any confederate – save, of course, that precious housekeeper of his. When I paced one corridor and found it six feet shorter than the corresponding one below, it was pretty clear where he was."

Holmes then explained the thumb mark, showing how when those packets were sealed up, Oldacre got McFarlane to secure a seal by putting his thumb upon the soft wax. Then he made an impression of this and moistened it with his own blood!

Such a cruel crime, to simultaneously frame the child of his lost fiancée and also swindle his creditors by paying cheques to himself under the name Mr Cornelius!

"But", said Holmes, "he had not that supreme gift of the artist – the knowledge of when to stop."

THE ADVENTURE OF THE PRIORY SCHOOL

THURSDAY, 16 MAY TO SATURDAY, 18 MAY 1901

Doctor Thorneycroft Alexander Ulysses Huxtable
B.A., B.Sc, M.A., Ph.D.Lit , Ph.D.Sc,
Magna Cum Laude, Fellow of Brasenose College Oxford,
Sponsor of the Harrow Scholarship of Brasenose College Oxford.

Founder And Principal

THE PRIORY
PREPARATORY SCHOOL
✦ MACKLETON ✦

↑ *Huxtable's card could barely hold the weight of the distinctions lavished upon it.*

We have had some dramatic entrances and exits upon our small stage at Baker Street, but I cannot recollect anything more sudden and startling than the first appearance of Thorneycroft Huxtable, MA, PhD, etc.

"I came personally, Mr Holmes, in order to ensure that you would return with me. Have you heard nothing of the abduction of the only son of the Duke of Holdernesse?

"I may tell you that His Grace has said that a cheque for five thousand pounds will be handed over to the person who can tell him where his son is, and another thousand for the abductor's identity.

"The Priory is the best preparatory school in England. Three weeks ago, the Duke sent Mr James Wilder, his secretary, to commit young Lord Arthur Saltire, ten years old, his only son and heir, to my charge."

Huxtable breathlessly proceeded to relate to us how at seven o'clock on Tuesday morning it was discovered that the boy had dressed and gone sometime in the night, evidently climbing down the ivy outside his window. Furthermore, Heidegger, the silent, morose German master, had also disappeared, although in a state of evident undress, along with his bicycle. A false sighting of a man and boy led to the proper investigation being delayed by three days.

"I will order a four-wheeler," said Holmes. "In a quarter of an hour we shall be at your service."

154 H

HOLDERNESSE, 6th Duke, K.G., P.C., G.C.B., K.C.M.G.

Baron Beverley, Earl of Carston. Lord Lieutenant of Hallamshire since 1900. Married Edith, daughter of Sir Charles Appledore, 1888. Heir and only child, Lord Saltire. Owns about two hundred and fifty thousand acres. Minerals in Lancashire and Wales. Address: Carlton House Terrace; Holdernesse Hall, Hallamshire; Carston Castle, Bangor, Wales. Lord of the Admiralty, 1872; Chief Secretary of State for

← *Lord Arthur Saltire seemed a fine if somewhat inward-looking young man.*

It was already dark when we reached The Priory School, but we swiftly learned that the Duke and his secretary had also arrived and wished to see us.

The Duke was a tall and stately person, scrupulously dressed. Beside him stood a small, nervous young man: Wilder, the private secretary.

Holmes questioned the Duke thoroughly, and took notes of key points.

The Duke then left for Holdernesse Hall, leaving us to investigate the scene of the alleged crime, which unfortunately yielded no further evidence whatsoever.

Holmes next went out to investigate the nearby area, and returned after 11 with a map of the neighbourhood.

By his distinctive process of elimination he managed to narrow the most likely area for the fugitives' flight, the desolate plain to the north, with Holdernesse Hall itself only six miles away across the moor.

Suddenly Dr Huxtable returned, bearing a blue cricket cap. It was apparently found in the caravan of gypsies camped on the moor, and despite their protestations that they had found it, they had been locked up to extract further information. Holmes was doubtful of their guilt but pleased this proved his moor theory, and we resolved to look there at first light tomorrow.

- Estranged from Duchess but does not think her responsible.
- Has not received any demands. Curious.
- Wrote to his son the day before but does not think the contents potentially unbalancing.
- Wrote 20 to 30 other letters that day, which were all posted by Mr James Wilder.

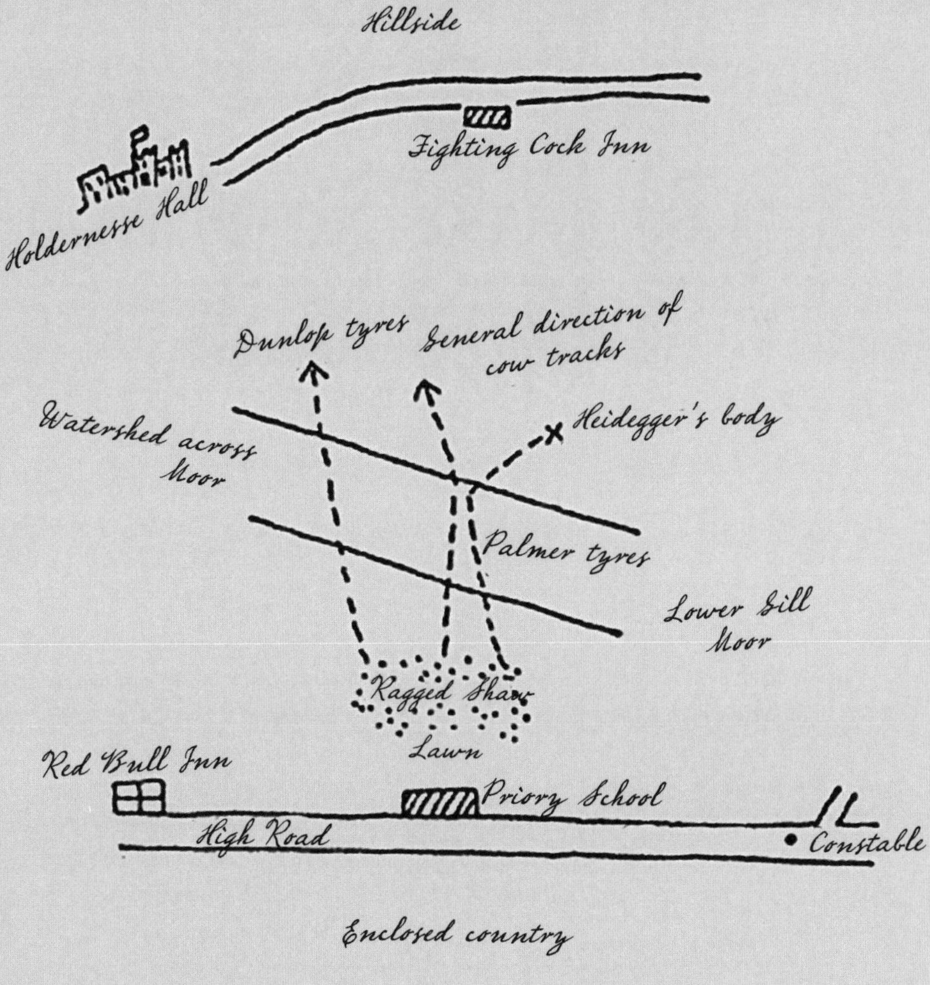

Hillside

Fighting Cock Inn

Holdernesse Hall

Dunlop tyres

General direction of cow tracks

Heidegger's body

Watershed across Moor

Palmer tyres

Lower Gill Moor

Ragged Shaw

Lawn

Red Bull Inn

Priory School

High Road

Constable

Enclosed country

↑ *Holmes' map was, as usual, imprecise but unquestionably correct.*

↑ *Bicycle tracks, several for analysis.*

The next day we struck across the moor, intersected with a thousand sheep paths, until we came to a broad, light-green belt marking the morass between us and Holdernesse. At first we found nothing but sheep marks and cow tracks, then lit on the track of a bicycle! But not the correct bicycle.

"I am familiar with 42 different impressions left by tyres," said Holmes. "This is a Dunlop. Heidegger's tyres were Palmer."

Further on, however, we did find Palmer tracks, partially eliminated by cow prints. We followed them, and came upon the bike itself, mangled and smeared with blood, and just next to it, its unfortunate rider… Heidegger's body, his skull partially crushed by a frightful blow.

"It is clear now", said Holmes, "that from his bedroom window, he saw the flight of the boy and wished to overtake him and bring him back. He seized his bicycle, pursued the lad, and in pursuing him met his death."

But there were no other marks, no bicycles or even human footprints, to suggest the boy or the murderer.

Following the Dunlop tracks, we found ourselves at the Fighting Cock inn. Holmes tested the landlord, a Mr Reuben Hayes, first by offering a sovereign for the use of a bicycle (Hayes claimed he had none) and then by seeing his reaction to the news that we were on the young Lord's track.

We sat down to a short meal in the stone-clad kitchen and Holmes casually asked if I found it strange there would be so many cow tracks and yet no cows evident...

"Can you recall that the tracks were sometimes like that, Watson," – he arranged a number of bread-crumbs into patterns – "and sometimes like this, and occasionally like this?"

I owned that I could not, and with a smile Holmes led me to the inn's tumbledown stable, where he showed that one of the unkempt horses there had "old shoes, but new nails"!

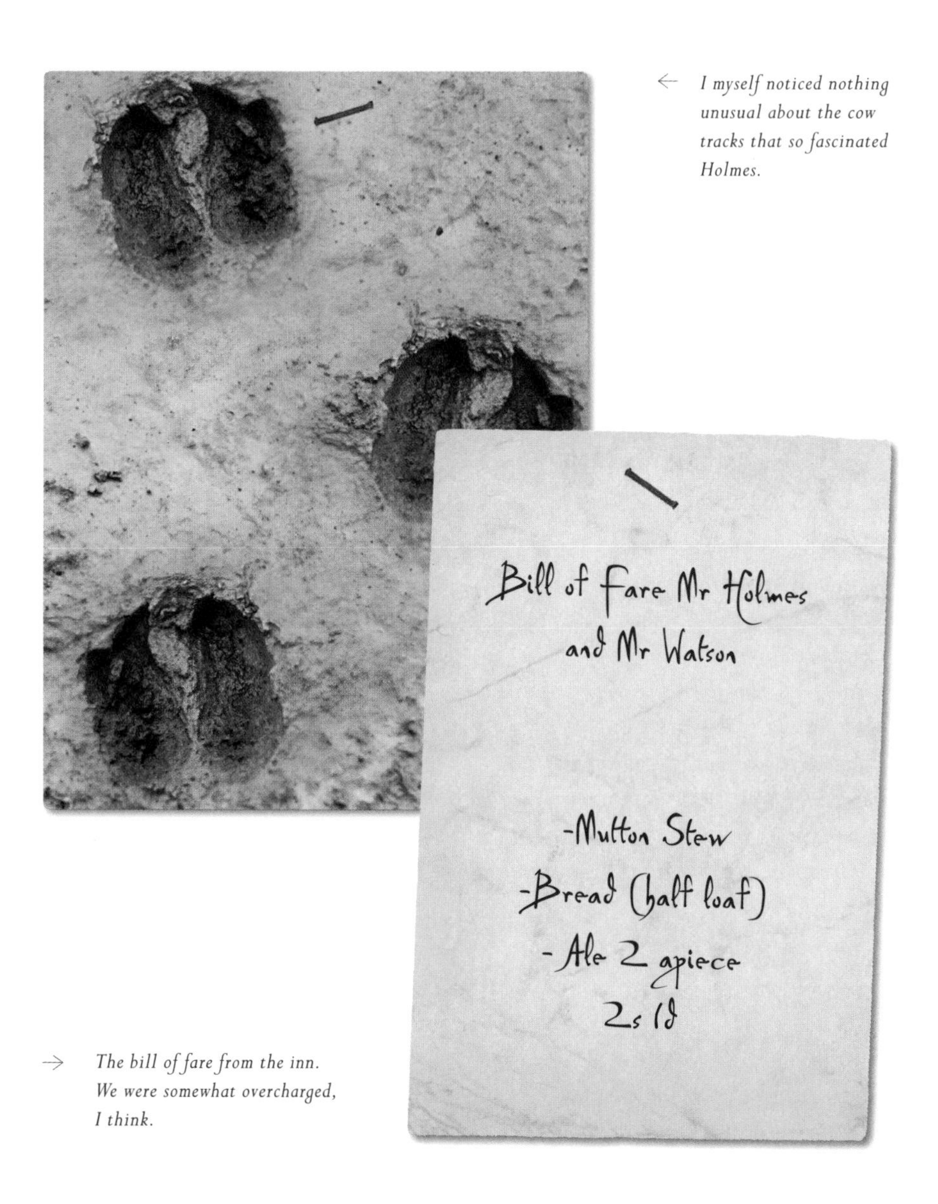

Bill of Fare Mr Holmes
and Mr Watson

-Mutton Stew
-Bread (half loaf)
-Ale 2 apiece
2s 1d

← *I myself noticed nothing unusual about the cow tracks that so fascinated Holmes.*

→ *The bill of fare from the inn. We were somewhat overcharged, I think.*

→ *The Fighting Cock had a long, if not illustrious, history.*

On finding us in his stable the landlord was very agitated, but when Mr Holmes questioned his unwarranted anger he mastered himself and asked us to leave.

"Yes, it is an interesting place, this Fighting Cock," said Holmes as we walked away. "I think we shall have another look at it in an unobtrusive way."

We had turned off the road, and were making our way up the hill, when Holmes suddenly threw me to the ground. Seconds later a very agitated-looking James Wilder flew past us on the road, riding a bicycle!

Circling round to secretly watch the front door of the inn, we saw his bicycle propped there, and then a horse and trap wheel out into the road and tear off in the direction of Chesterfield.

Carefully we moved forward and Holmes inspected the bicycle by match-light, to find the Dunlop tyres we sought.

After a brief look over an adjoining wall (aided by my shoulders), Holmes declared our day's work done, and we returned to the school.

At 11 o'clock next morning my friend and I were walking up the famous yew avenue of Holdernesse Hall. We were ushered into His Grace's study. There we found Mr James Wilder, demure and courtly, but with some trace of that wild terror of the night before still lurking in his furtive eyes and twitching features. He seemed very reluctant to permit us access to the Duke but eventually relented, and upon seeing him Holmes spoke rapidly.

"I see Your Grace's chequebook upon the table," said he. "I should be glad if you would make me out a cheque for five thousand pounds."

"Where is my son?" he gasped.

"He is, or was last night, at the Fighting Cock inn."

"And whom do you accuse?"

"I accuse you," said he. "And now, Your Grace, I'll trouble you for that cheque."

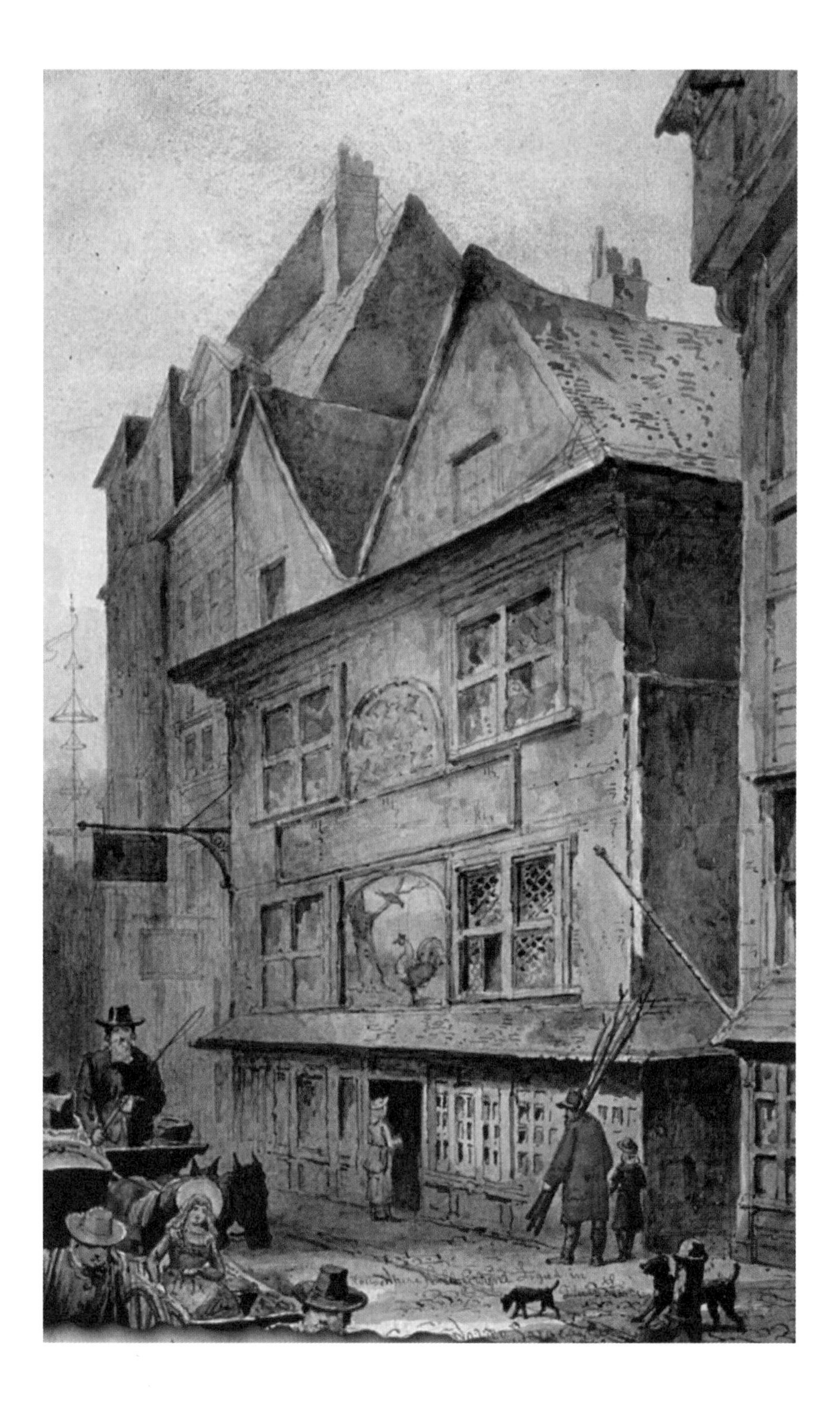

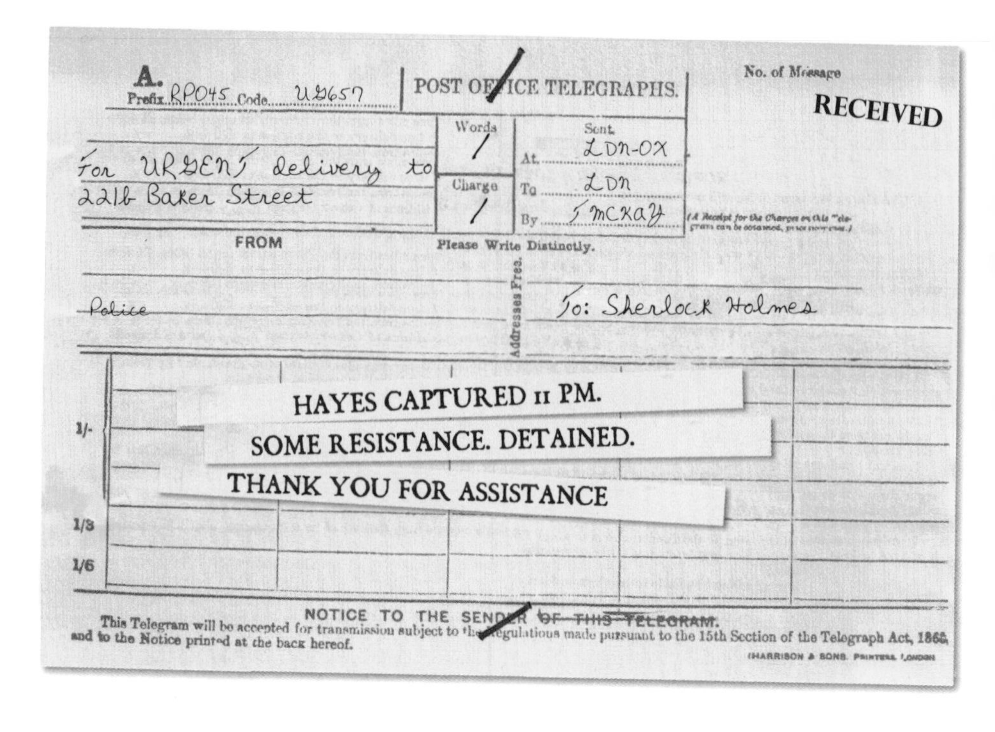

A.
Prefix RPO45 Code U2657

POST OFFICE TELEGRAPHS.

No. of Message

RECEIVED

Words 1
Charge 1

Sent
At LDN-OX
To LDN
By J McKay

(A Receipt for the Charges on this Telegram can be obtained, price one penny.)

For URGENT delivery to
221b Baker Street

FROM
Police

Please Write Distinctly.

Addresses Free.

To: Sherlock Holmes

1/-
1/3
1/6

HAYES CAPTURED 11 PM.
SOME RESISTANCE. DETAINED.
THANK YOU FOR ASSISTANCE

NOTICE TO THE SENDER OF THIS TELEGRAM.
This Telegram will be accepted for transmission subject to the Regulations made pursuant to the 15th Section of the Telegraph Act, 1868, and to the Notice printed at the back hereof.

HARRISON & SONS. PRINTERS, LONDON

The Duke sprang up and clawed with his hands like one who is sinking into an abyss. Then, with extraordinary effort, he sat down and sank his face in his hands.

"How much do you know?" he asked at last, without raising his head.

"I saw you together last night."

"Does anyone else besides your friend know?"

"I have spoken to no one."

The Duke subtly implied he might double the amount in exchange for total discretion, but Holmes insisted the death of the German master made this impossible.

"But James knew nothing of that, it was the work of this brutal ruffian whom he had the misfortune to employ. The instant that he heard of it he made a complete confession to me, and lost not an hour in breaking entirely with the murderer!"

"Mr Reuben Hayes was arrested at Chesterfield on my information at 11 o'clock last night," added Holmes reassuringly. "I had a telegram from the head of the local police before I left the school this morning."

"I am right glad to hear it," said the Duke, "if it will not react upon the fate of James."

"Your secretary?"

"No, sir; my son."

It was Holmes' turn to look astonished.

I am reluctant to relate fully the circumstances of James Wilder's origins, but it was a matter of a fierce young love that was nonetheless a poor match, and then when the mother died the Duke took the child under his wing as much he could, unable to acknowledge his paternity. Of course, Wilder resented the young Lord and this may have led the Duke and Duchess to part. In the end the Duke sent Lord Saltire to The Priory for what he felt was his own safety.

"That evening James bicycled over," the Duke continued "and told Arthur that his mother longed to see him, was waiting on the moor, and that if he came back at midnight he would find a man with a horse, who would take him to her. Poor Arthur fell into the trap. He found Hayes and they set off together. They were pursued, Hayes struck, and the man died. Hayes brought Arthur to the Fighting Cock, where he was confined in an upper room, under the care of Mrs Hayes."

Wilder confessed but begged the Duke keep the secret for three more days to permit him to inform Hayes and aid his escape. Holmes was scathing of this decision and pointed out the Duke had condoned a felony, but acquiesced upon learning that James Wilder would be dispatched to Australia to seek his fortune there.

There was one last point. "Hayes shod his horses with shoes which counterfeited the tracks of cows. Was this from Mr Wilder?"

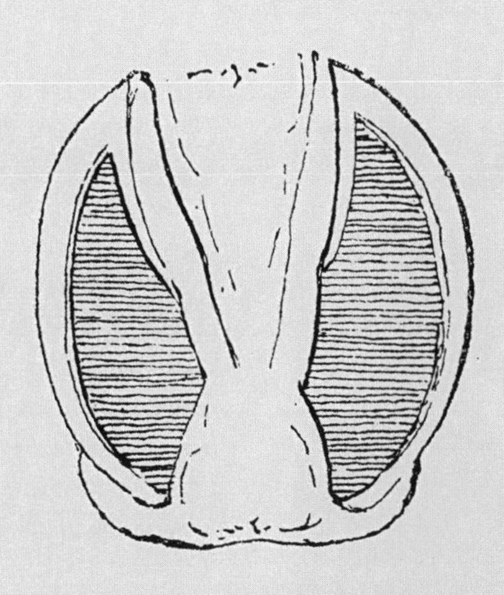

↑ *A diagram of the ingenious horse shoes I detail on the next page.*

Lord Saltire

I apologise for using this clandestine method of contact, but it is vital that I impart information to you regarding your mother, the Duchess, not to be known by your father. Please meet me at the Ragged Shaw (I'm sure you're aware it is a little wood near the school at approximately eight in the evening.

Once again I beg that you tell no one of this meeting.

Yours respectfully,

James Wilder

← *Wilder's false note has an air of desperation to it.*

↙ *Wilder's banishment ultimately proved best for everyone involved.*

The Duke led us to a small personal museum and indicated a case.

"These shoes were dug up in the moat of Holdernesse Hall. They are for the use of horses; but they are shaped below with a cloven foot of iron, so as to throw pursuers off the track. They belonged to some of the marauding Barons of Holdernesse in the Middle Ages."

"Thank you," said Holmes, as he replaced the glass. "It is the second-most interesting object that I have seen in the North."

The first, he suggested, was the cheque.

THE PRIORY SCHOOL MACKLETON

REPORT

Name: *Arthur Saltire* | *1901*

Attendance	10	STUDIES		EXTRA STUDIES	
Neatness	9	Scripture	10	French grammar	10
Deportment	9	Orthography	7	Greek classics	10
		Definitions	10	Latin	10
		Reading	9		
		Grammar	9		
		Modern Geography	10		
		Practical Arithmetic	9		
		Algebra	8		
		History	8		
		English	9		
		English Literature	10		
		Mythology	9		
		Geometry	7		
		Theology	10		
		Physical exercise	9		

Principal's observations:

It would appear from his marks that Arthur is a promising student with no little ability showing progress in many of his studies. On a personal note I have found him a pleasant and personable young fellow. However we must be watchful and make sure that the recent events at home do not become too much of a burden on his young shoulders. To this end I have placed him under the wing of one of the senior boys.

Dr. Thorneycroft Huxtable.

↑ *Arthur Saltire's favourable report from the Priory School, Mackleton.*

THE ADVENTURE OF THE SOLITARY CYCLIST

TUESDAY, 23 APRIL TO SATURDAY, 4 MAY 1895

The Times

For The Attention Of Mrs Enid Smith or Miss Violet Smith, if they or anyone who can speak to their whereabouts can contact Mr Robert Fender of Fender, Gilbey and Freedman, 13 Haymarket, London, they will find it very beneficial to them.

The mysterious advertisement.

23 April 1895: the young and beautiful Miss Violet Smith presented herself at Baker Street late in the evening and implored Holmes's assistance.

"At least it cannot be your health," said he, as his keen eyes darted over her. "So ardent a bicyclist must be full of energy."

She glanced down in surprise at her own feet, and I observed the slight roughening of the side of the sole caused by the friction of the edge of the pedal.

"Yes, and that has something to do with my visit to you today."

My friend took the lady's ungloved hand. "You observe the spatulate finger-end, Watson, which is common to both typists and pianists? There is a spirituality about the face, however, which the typewriter does not generate. You are a musician."

She nodded, then continued. "My late father was James Smith, who conducted the orchestra at the old Imperial Theatre. My only remaining relatives are my mother and one uncle Ralph Smith, who went to Africa 25 years ago and has never been heard from again. We are poor, but four months ago there was an advertisement in The Times *enquiring for our whereabouts. We thought that perhaps someone had left us a fortune!"*

"As a result we met two gentlemen, Mr Carruthers and Mr Woodley, who were home on a visit from South Africa. They said that my uncle was a friend of theirs, who had died some months before in great poverty in Johannesburg, but had asked them with his last breath to hunt up his relations and see that they were in no want."

"Mr Woodley was an odious person, making eyes at me, and I was sure my fiancé, Cyril Morton, would not approve. Mr Carruthers was much older but more agreeable. Dark and sallow but with polite manners and a pleasant smile. On finding that we were very poor, he suggested that I should come and teach music to his only daughter, aged ten. We drew up an extremely fair agreement."

"All was well until Mr Woodley arrived for a visit of a week, and oh, it seemed three months to me! He pursued and harassed me endlessly, and finally, when I would have nothing to do with him, he seized me in his arms and swore that he would not let me go until I had kissed him. Mr Carruthers came in and tore him off from me, on which Mr Woodley turned upon his host, knocking him down and cutting his face open. I saw him no more."

But the strangest thing, she explained, was that recently she'd become aware of another cyclist following her on her regular rides to and from the station,

A. Prefix LDN1 Code DAR23

POST OFFICE TELEGRAPHS.

No. of Message

For swift delivery

Words: 5

Charge: 1-/3d

Sent At: Plnt P.O

To: GR1M11

By: P. Derry

(A Receipt for the Charges on this Telegram can be obtained, price one penny.)

FROM

Cyril Janney,
Johannesberg, South Africa

Please Write Distinctly.

Addresses Free.

Tobias Woodley,
Charlington Hall, Farnham

The	old	man	is	dead.

1/-

1/3

1/6

NOTICE TO THE SENDER ~~OF THIS TELEGRAM~~.
This Telegram will be accepted for transmission subject to the Regulations made pursuant to the 15th Section of the Telegraph Act, 1868, and to the Notice printed at the back hereof.

HARRISON & SONS. PRINTERS, LONDON

a man with a short, dark beard. One time, out of curiosity, she waited round a corner for him to shoot past, but although there was no turning off the road, he disappeared! With his swift intelligence, Holmes deduced that the man could only have come from nearby Charlington Hall.

Holmes' final query was about Carruthers' career and monetary status, and although Miss Smith was sure he was rich, she could not name his employment and believed he did not even have a horse.

CONTRACT OF EMPLOYMENT

On this day, the 7th February 1895, it is agreed that Miss Violet Smith will live at Chiltern Grange, Farnham, and while there will instruct Miss Amanda Carruthers in the practice of piano playing and any other musical instruction that is deemed necessary. For this she will be paid the sum of £100 per annum. She will furthermore be permitted to leave the Grange at weekends for the purpose of visiting her mother.

Signed by

V. Smith Robert Carruthers

Miss Violet Smith and Mr Robert Carruthers

↑ *Miss Smith's agreement seemed fair on the surface.*

↑ *As with many things, Holmes had published several papers on beards as disguises.*

After she had left, Holmes commented, "Our first effort must be to find who are the tenants of Charlington Hall. And what is the connection between Carruthers and Woodley? Furthermore, what sort of a ménage pays double the market price for a governess, but does not keep a horse although six miles from the station?"

It was agreed that I would go to Farnham, conceal myself near Charlington Heath and witness what occurred.

I travelled there and hid myself behind a clump of flowering gorse, and sure enough a darkly bearded man arrived and concealed himself in a gap in the hedge. A quarter of an hour later Miss Smith passed on her bicycle, and the man emerged and began to follow her. Once again, on this day she decided to whirl round and challenge him; it was only his swiftness that allowed his escape. I could find no trace of him.

Then, directed by a house agent in Farnham, I proceeded to a firm in Pall Mall, who insisted that Charlington Hall was let to Mr Williamson, a respectable elderly gentleman.

When I reported back to Holmes, his only comment was to admonish me for visiting a house agent when a much better result could be had from the local public house!

Next morning we had a note from Miss Smith, recounting shortly and accurately the very incidents that I had seen, but the pith of the letter lay in the postscript:

P.S. I am sure that you will respect my confidence, Mr Holmes, when I tell you that my place here has become difficult owing to the fact that my employer has proposed marriage to me. I am convinced that his feelings are most deep and most honourable. At the same time my promise is, of course, given. He took my refusal very seriously, but also very gently. You can understand, however, that the situation is a little strained.

"Our young friend seems to be getting into deep waters," said Holmes thoughtfully, and decided to conduct his own investigations this time.

Holmes' "quiet day in the country" had a singular termination, for he arrived at Baker Street late in the evening with a cut lip and a discoloured lump upon his forehead. He was immensely tickled by his own adventures, and laughed heartily as he recounted them.

"I found that country pub which I had already recommended to your notice, and there I made my discreet enquiries. I was in the bar, and a garrulous landlord was giving me all that I wanted. Williamson is a white-bearded man, and he lives alone with a small staff of servants at the Hall. There is some rumour that he is or has been a clergyman!" (Holmes had later made enquiries at a clerical agency, who told him there was a man of that name in orders who had a dark career.)

"The landlord described several visitors, but the permanent resident is our erstwhile Mr Woodley! Then who should walk in but the gentleman himself, who had been drinking his beer in the taproom and had heard the whole conversation. He launched a string of abusive questions followed by a vicious backhander, which I failed to entirely avoid. The next few minutes were delicious. It was a straight left against a slogging ruffian. I emerged as you see me. Mr Woodley went home in a cart. So ended my country trip!"

← *Miss Smith felt uncomfortable about her employer's proposal*

↑ *Another case, another confrontation in an inn...*

↑ *Many underestimate Holmes' skills as a pugilist.*

The Thursday brought us another letter from our client. It revealed that she would be leaving Carruthers' service on Saturday due to the unwanted reappearance of the now rather disfigured Mr Woodley, slinking around outside the property like a wild animal.

"It is our duty to see that no one molests her upon that last journey. I think, Watson, that we must spare time to run down together on Saturday morning, and make sure that this curious and inconclusive investigation has no untoward ending."

Mr S. Holmes and Dr J. Watson
221b Baker Street
London

Dear Mr Holmes and Dr Watson,

You will not be surprised, Mr. Holmes, to hear that I am leaving Mr Carruthers's employment. Even the high pay cannot reconcile me to the discomforts of my situation. On Saturday, I come up to town and I do not intend to return. Mr Carruthers has got a trap, and so the dangers of the lonely road, if there ever were any dangers, are now over.

As to the special cause of my leaving, it is not merely the strained situation with Mr Carruthers, but it is the reappearance of that odious man, Mr Woodley. He was always hideous, but he looks more awful than ever now, for he appears to have had an accident and he is much disfigured. I saw him out of the window, but I am glad to say I

↑ *Miss Smith was driven from her place by Mr Woodley's behaviour*

did not meet him. He had a long talk with Mr Carruthers, who seemed much excited afterwards. Woodley must be staying in the neighbourhood, for he did not sleep here, and yet I caught a glimpse of him again this morning slinking about in the shrubbery. I would sooner have a savage wild animal loose about the place. I loathe and fear him more than I can say. How can Mr Carruthers endure such a creature for a moment? However, all my troubles will be over on Saturday.

Yours sincerely,

Miss Violet Smith

I confess that I had not taken a serious view of the case, which had seemed to me rather grotesque and bizarre than dangerous. It was the severity of Holmes' manner, and the revolver he pocketed before leaving our rooms, which impressed me with the feeling that tragedy might occur.

Holmes and I walked along the broad, sandy road inhaling the fresh morning air. A pony trap, possibly Miss Smith's, moved towards us, but at the next moment we could not see it. Holmes broke into a run. As we approached the spot, an empty dog cart, the reins trailing, appeared round the curve of the road and rattled swiftly towards us.

"Too late, Watson; too late!" cried Holmes, entreating me to block the horse and climb in, and we set off to find the possibly abducted Miss Smith. It was then that we glimpsed the Solitary Cyclist, who charged angrily towards us and drew a pistol from his pocket.

"Pull up, I say, or, by George, I'll put a bullet into your horse!"

"You're the man we want to see. Where is Miss Violet Smith?" Holmes said, in his quick, clear way.

"That's what I should ask you, you're in her dog cart!"

We explained how we had found it empty and he looked horrified. "Good Lord!" cried the stranger. "They've got her, that hellhound Woodley and the blackguard parson!"

We left the trap and all three of us followed tracks to find Peter, the trap's groom, clubbed and bloodied but alive in the bushes.

A woman's shrill scream burst from bushes in front of us, ending on its highest note with a choke and a gurgle. We broke through. Under a mighty oak stood three people. One was a woman, our client, drooping and faint, a handkerchief round her mouth. Opposite her, the red-moustached Mr Woodley. Between them an elderly, grey-bearded man had evidently just completed the wedding service.

"They're married!" I gasped.

Woodley spotted the bearded man and laughed.

"You can take your beard off, Bob," said he.

He ripped it off and brought his revolver up.

"Yes, I am Bob Carruthers. I told you what I'd do if you molested her, and, by the Lord, I'll be as good as my word!"

"You're too late. She's my wife!"

"No, she's your widow."

His revolver cracked, and I saw the blood spurt from the front of Woodley's waistcoat as he collapsed backwards.

Everyone, including Carruthers, was shocked, and Holmes took charge. Carruthers and the clergyman Williamson found themselves carrying the wounded Woodley into Charlington Hall, and I gave my arm to the frightened girl.

The resolution was prolonged but overdue. Holmes quickly admonished the defrocked vicar and declared the "marriage" to be a sham.

"You and Woodley knew Ralph Smith in South Africa," surmised Holmes. "He had amassed a considerable fortune. You had reason to believe that he would not live long and realized that his niece

↖ *We had arrived just in the nick of time.*

18*95*. Marriage solemnized at *S. Philip Church* in the

No.	When Married.	Name and Surname.	Age.	Custodian.	Ra
108	*4th May* 18*95*	*Mr Tobias Woodley*	*33*	*Widower*	
		Miss Violet Smith	*28*	*Tutor*	

Married in the *Church of St Philip* according to the Rites and Cerem

This Marriage was solemnized between us, { *Mr Tobias Woodley* / *Miss Violet Smith* } in the Presence of us, {

I.O.U. Violet Smith

↑ *A shabby souvenir of a shabby agreement.*

of Farnham in the County of Surrey

n.	Residence at the time of Marriage.	Father's Name and Surname.	Rank or Profession of Father.
	Charlington Hall	William Woodley	Farmer
	Chiltern Grange, Farnham	James Smith	Orchestra Conductor

English Church by or after by me,

Arthur Mann Charles Weldon

Alan Nott

would inherit his fortune."

Carruthers nodded shamefully.

"So you came over, and hunted up the girl. One of you would marry her, the other share the plunder. Woodley was chosen as the husband. Why?"

"We played cards for her on the voyage. He won."

But Carruthers fell in love with Miss Smith and sought to secretly protect her from Woodley, hence the bicycle and beard. The situation accelerated when they received a telegram from South Africa.

"I think that you have done what you could to make amends for your share in an evil plot," conceded Holmes, offering Carruthers his card for evidence during any trial.

After this point all that is left to be said is Miss Violet Smith did inherit a large fortune, and married Cyril Morton. Williamson and Woodley were both tried for abduction and assault, the former getting seven years and the latter ten. Of the fate of Carruthers I have no record, but I imagine that a few months were sufficient to satisfy the demands of justice.

THE ADVENTURE OF BLACK PETER

WEDNESDAY, 3 JULY 1895

During the first week of July, several rough-looking men called and enquired for Captain Basil, so I understood Holmes was working somewhere under one of his numerous disguises and names.

I had just sat down to breakfast when Holmes strode into the room with a huge barb-headed spear tucked like an umbrella under his arm.

The reason for this insanity became clear with the arrival of Stanley Hopkins, a young police inspector for whose future Holmes had high hopes. He had sadly made no progress in the intriguing murder of the man known as Black Peter, a case he had shared with Holmes.

Black Peter's household consisted of his wife, daughter and servants, but he slept in a wooden outhouse fashioned to look like a ship's cabin. He was a violent, unpleasant drunkard. That night he had raged and screamed in his customary way, so no one thought anything of it before he was discovered in the morning.

"Well, I have fairly steady nerves, as you know, Mr Holmes," said Hopkins, "but I give you my word that I got a shake at what I saw. It was droning like a harmonium with flies, and the floor and walls were like a slaughterhouse. Right through his broad breast a steel harpoon had been driven, and sunk deep into the wood of the wall behind him. Pinned like a beetle on a card!"

Captain Peter Carey. Born 5th January 1845.

1867 Seal and whale fisher, various ships, successful

1883 commanded the steam sealer Sea Unicorn, of Dundee.

Conducted several successful voyages

1884 Retired.

1884–1889 travelled world

1889–1895 Bought Woodman's Lee nr Forest Row in Sussex, lived there until murder

↑ *Hopkins' notes coldly reduced Carey's life to a series of events.*

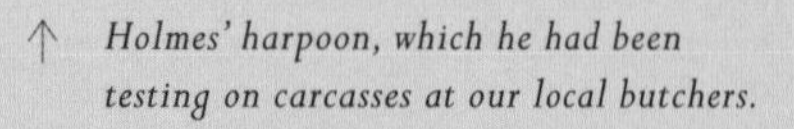

↑ *Holmes' harpoon, which he had been testing on carcasses at our local butchers.*

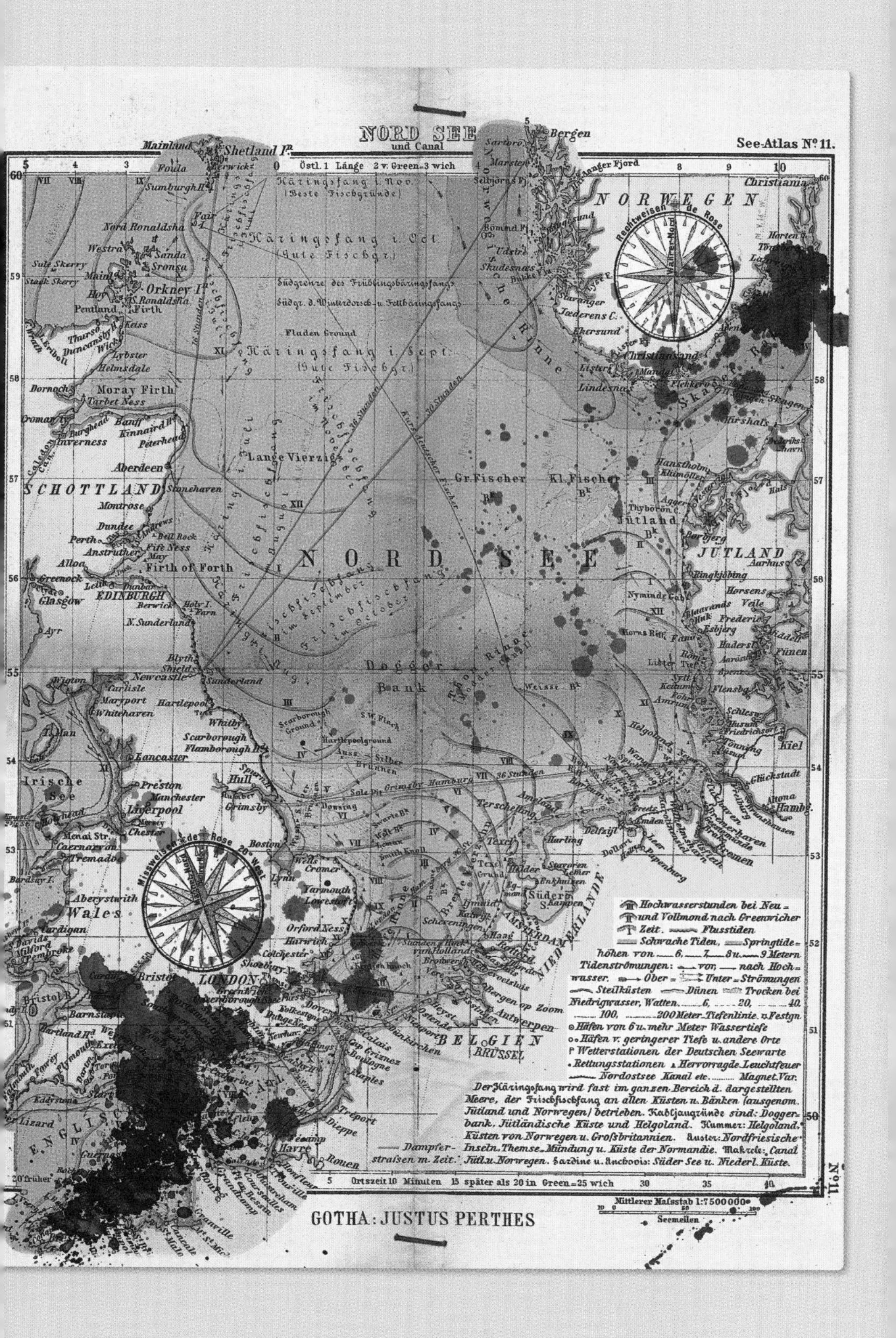
NORD SEE
und Canal
See-Atlas No. 11.
Shetland I.
Bergen
NORWEGEN
Christiania
Orkney I.
Moray Firth
Aberdeen
SCHOTTLAND
Firth of Forth
EDINBURGH
Glasgow
Newcastle
Sunderland
NORD SEE
Dogger Bank
Lange Vierzig
Gr. Fischer
Kl. Fischer
Jütland
JUTLAND
Helgoland
Kiel
Hamb.
Bremen
Hull
Liverpool
Manchester
Irische See
Wales
Bristol
LONDON
Amsterdam
NIEDERLANDE
BELGIEN
BRÜSSEL
Antwerpen
Calais
Boulogne
Dieppe
Havre
Rouen
Rechtweisende Rose
Missweisende Rose
Der Häringsfang wird fast im ganzen Bereich d. dargestellten Meere, der Frischfischfang an allen Küsten u. Bänken (ausgenom. Jütland und Norwegen) betrieben. Kabljaugründe sind: Doggerbank, Jütländische Küste und Helgoland. Hummer: Helgoland, Küsten von Norwegen u. Grossbritannien. Auster: Nordfriesische Inseln, Themse-Mündung u. Küste der Normandie. Makrele: Canal Jütl. u. Norwegen. Sardine u. Anchovis: Süder See u. Niederl. Küste.
Ortszeit 10 Minuten 15 später als 20 in Green. = 25 wich
Mittlerer Massstab 1:7500000
Seemeilen
GOTHA: JUSTUS PERTHES

↓ *A picture of the* Sea Unicorn *from the National Archives.*

SUSSEX POLICE

East Grinstead **STATION** Arthur Slater, Stonemason **WITNESS**

It was Monday and I was walking from Forest Row about one o'clock in the morning – like usual, when I see this shadow in the window of his cabin, and it weren't him, I knew him. He had a beard but it was shorter than Peter's. I wasn't drunk despite what some might say, I was in the pub before, but I saw it clear as day. I reckon that's the fellow what done him.

↑ → *Hopkins' report and notes.*

Two days before the murder there had been a witness…

Hopkins showed us the report, notes on the scene and items found, including a notebook. Holmes examined the notebook.

"'CPR' could be Canadian Pacific Railway," said he.

Stanley Hopkins swore between his teeth and struck his thigh with his clenched hand. Of course it is!" he cried. "Then 'JHN' are the only initials we have to solve."

Holmes furthermore deduced that the bloodstain on the book meant it was most likely dropped by the murderer in his flight from the cabin.

Holmes was lost in thought for some time.

"Well," said he, at last, "I suppose I shall have to come out and have a look at it."

Stanley Hopkins gave a cry of joy.

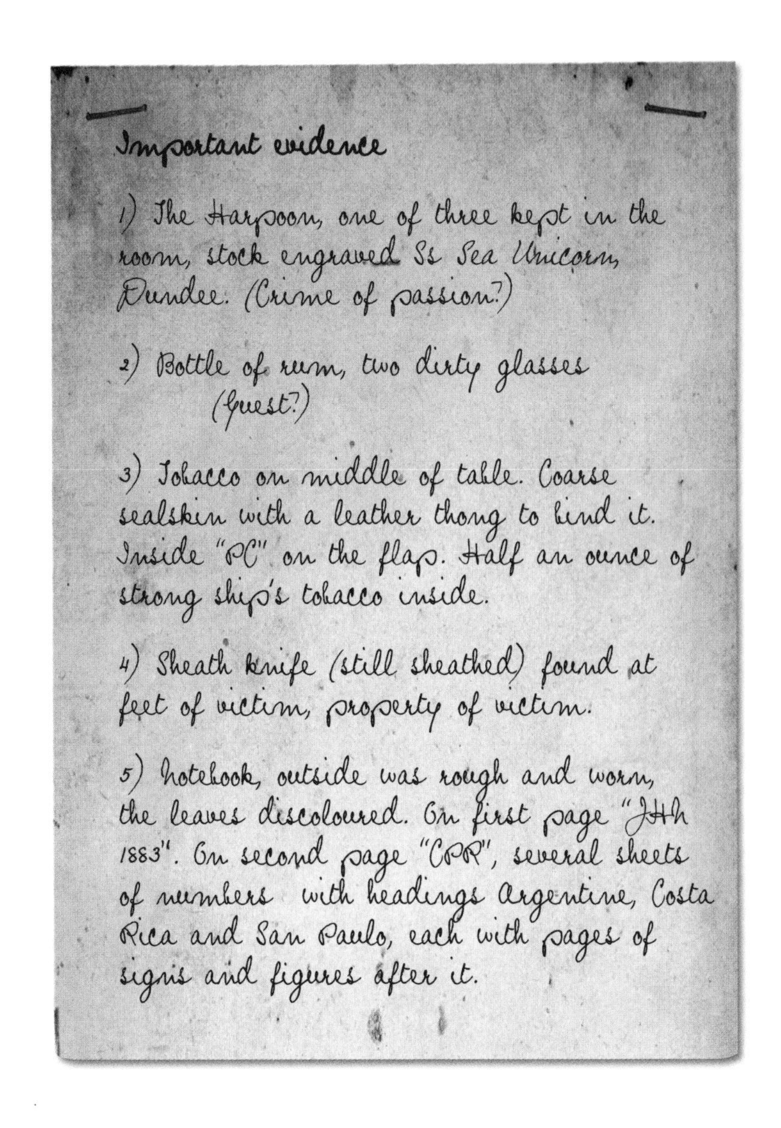

Important evidence

1) The Harpoon, one of three kept in the room, stock engraved Ss Sea Unicorn, Dundee. (Crime of passion?)

2) Bottle of rum, two dirty glasses (Guest?)

3) Tobacco on middle of table. Coarse sealskin with a leather thong to bind it. Inside "PC" on the flap. Half an ounce of strong ship's tobacco inside.

4) Sheath knife (still sheathed) found at feet of victim, property of victim.

5) Notebook, outside was rough and worn, the leaves discoloured. On first page "JHN 1883". On second page "CPR", several sheets of numbers with headings Argentine, Costa Rica and San Paulo, each with pages of signs and figures after it.

56 Daily Telegraph

NEEDED – Skilled harpooners to undertake 2-month Arctic expedition under Captain Basil Shenton, experienced seafarer of 35 years. The going will be hard but the rewards significant, a fair share of the profits for every man guaranteed and certified before the voyage commences.
All those interested, please contact Bates, Edward and Sons at 176 Gray's Inn Road, London.
Only serious applicants please.

TO RENT – A three story house, located on Mount Street, London, a few doors from the church. This house is well calculated to accommodate a genteel family and is in good repair. The terms may be known upon application to John Edwards, Esq.

↑ *A newspaper advertisement for skilled harpooners, placed by Sherlock Holmes under the guise of Captain Basil Shenton.*

Alighting at the small wayside station, we drove for some miles through the remains of widespread woods.

Stanley Hopkins led us first to the house, where he introduced the widow of the victim, whose gaunt and deep-lined face and furtive look of terror told of her years of hardship and ill usage. Her daughter, a pale, fair-haired girl, told us that she was glad that her father was dead, and that she blessed the hand which had struck him down.

On approaching the cabin Hopkins realized someone had attempted to force the lock in the interim. This pleased Holmes greatly, as he had suspected the culprit would return.

On inspecting the cabin he found a further anomaly: "Something has been taken. There is less dust in this corner of the shelf than elsewhere. It may have been a book lying on its side."

We arranged to meet Hopkins later, and form a little ambuscade to catch the fellow.

At past 11 p.m. we crouched amongst the bushes outside the cabin, and it was not until half past two in the morning that the burglar returned, a young man, frail and thin, barely 20 years old. He lit a candle and began feverishly reading through the logbooks in the cabin, gesturing angrily with each unsuccessful search, and he did not stop until Hopkins' hand was on his collar…

↓ *An excerpt from the logs Neligan had been searching so feverishly.*

Thursday April 5th 1883
12 days out
Today we are we off Cape Navarin with a light breeze. Seen our first ice today. This evening, sighted two ships, do not know who they are, think one is the Griffon, saw a few Walruses and Killers. First Mate and I have been mounting watches, had some good walks upon the deck.

Friday April 6th 1883
13 days out
A very fine day and a light breeze. Captain O'Dwyer of the Berkshire able to come aboard at seven o'clock and took breakfast with us. He brought us papers. We have been going through the ice, saw a few Walrus today.

"Now, my fine fellow," said Stanley Hopkins, "who are you, and what do you want here?"

"I am John Hopley Neligan," said the man with an effort at self-composure.

I saw Holmes and Hopkins exchange a quick glance.

"What are you doing here?"

"Did you ever hear of Dawson & Neligan?"

SEARCH FOR ARTHUR NELIGAN ENTERS EIGHTH DAY

HOPES ARE FADING FOR THE DISCOVERY of fugitive banker Arthur Neligan, whose yacht, reported as embarking for Norway on the 18th of this month, has evidently disappeared. Mr Neligan of Dawson & Neligan is alleged to have absconded with all the bank's securities after its recent failure caused the loss of a million pounds, bankrupting many prominent Cornwall county families. He boarded his yacht just after a warrant was issued for his arrest, but subsequent searches along his proposed route have yielded no sign.

↑ *The newspaper report on Neligan's father told a sad tale.*

"I believed my father and the securities were at the bottom of the sea. Then I learned that some of them had reappeared on the London market. You can imagine my amazement. Eventually, I discovered that the original seller had been Captain Peter Carey."

Neligan explained that he thought his father's yacht may have been blown to the north and somehow met with Carey's ship, the *Sea Unicorn*.

"I tried last night to get at these logbooks, but was unable to open the door. Tonight I tried again, and succeeded; but I find that the pages which deal with that month have been torn from the book."

He claimed not to have been there otherwise until Hopkins presented him with the bloodstained notebook, at which he collapsed and claimed he had lost it at the hotel. Hopkins took Neligan off to the police station, but Holmes said he felt there was an alternative explanation, though he did not state it.

↑ *Neligan did not have the swagger or the build of a harpoon murderer.*

Several letters were waiting for Holmes at Baker Street. He snatched one of them up, opened it, and burst out into a triumphant chuckle of laughter.

"Excellent, Watson. Have you telegraph forms? Just write a couple of messages for me."

Next morning, as requested, Inspector Stanley Hopkins appeared, in high spirits. He had refined his explanation of the murder, committed by Neligan in a fit of passion on confronting Peter Carey, then running and dropping the notebook.

"It seems to me to have only one drawback, Hopkins," said Holmes "Have you tried to drive a harpoon through a body? No? My friend Watson could tell you that I spent a whole morning in that exercise. Do you imagine that this anaemic youth was capable of so frightful an assault? Is he the man who drank rum with Black Peter? Was it his profile that was seen two nights before?"

Hopkins looked uncertain. "This terrible person of yours, where is he?"

"I rather fancy that he is on the stair," said Holmes, serenely. "I think, Watson, that you would do well to put that revolver where you can reach it."

Mrs Hudson then opened the door to say that there were three men enquiring for Captain Basil.

The first two, Holmes dismissed within a few sentences, paying each a half sovereign. The third had a fierce bulldog face framed in a tangle of hair and beard, and bold, dark eyes.

"Your name?" asked Holmes.

A. Prefix RPO45 Code U&657

POST OFFICE TELEGRAPHS.

No. of Message

URGENT

Words 9

Charge 1/-

Sent At LDN-OX To LDN By 5 McKAY

(A Receipt for the Charges on this Telegram can be obtained, price ...)

FROM — Please Write Distinctly.

Sherlock Holmes

Addresses Free.

Sumner, Shipping Agent, Ratcliff Highway.

	Send	three	men,	to	arrive
1/-	10a.m.	tomorrow.	- Basil.		
1/3					
1/6					

NOTICE TO THE SENDER ~~OF THIS TELEGRAM~~.
This Telegram will be accepted for transmission subject to the Regulations made pursuant to the 15th Section of the Telegraph Act, 1868, and to the Notice printed at the back hereof.

HARRISON & SONS. PRINTERS, LONDON

A. Prefix RP045 Code U2657

POST OFFICE TELEGRAPHS.

No. of Message

URGENT

Words 9

Charge 1/-

Sent. At LDN-OX

To LDN

By 5 MCKAY

(A Receipt for the Charges on this Telegram can be obtained, price one penny.)

FROM: Sherlock Holmes

Please Write Distinctly.

Addresses Pres.: Inspector Stanley Hopkins, 46, Lord Street, Brixton.

	Breakfast	tomorrow	9.30.	Important.	Wire
1/-	if	unable to		come.	- Sherlock
	Holmes				
1/3					
1/6					

NOTICE TO THE SENDER ~~OF THIS TELEGRAM.~~

This Telegram will be accepted for transmission subject to the Regulations made pursuant to the 15th Section of the Telegraph Act, 1868, and to the Notice printed at the back hereof.

HARRISON & SONS. PRINTERS, LONDON

"Patrick Cairns."

"Harpooner?"

"Yes, sir. Twenty-six voyages."

"Here's the agreement on the side table. If you sign it the whole matter will be settled."

"Shall I sign here?" the seaman asked, stooping over the table.

Holmes leaned over his shoulder and passed both hands over his neck.

"This will do," said he.

I heard a click of steel and a bellow like an enraged bull. The next instant Holmes and the seaman were rolling on the ground together. Even with the handcuffs which Holmes had fastened upon his wrists, he would have overpowered my friend had Hopkins and I not rushed to his rescue.

"I give you Patrick Cairns, the true murderer of Peter Carey."

"You say I murdered Peter Carey; I say I killed Peter Carey, and there's all the difference," objected the man from his position on the floor. "I knew Black Peter, and when he pulled out his knife I whipped a harpoon through him sharp, for I knew that it was him or me."

The harpooner related his tale, telling of how while working under Peter Carey on the Sea Unicorn they had picked up a man off the Norwegian coast in a dinghy. His only baggage was a tin box, and the next day the man had disappeared as if he had never been. Only Cairn had seen with his own eyes Carey tipping the man overboard.

Cairns had travelled to the cabin in order to put "the squeeze" on Carey for money, and their first meeting had been

congenial, but the second had brought them to violence and Carey's end.

Holmes nodded. "The amazing strength, the skill in the use of the harpoon, the rum and water, the sealskin tobacco-pouch, with the coarse tobacco – all these pointed to a seaman, and one who had been a whaler. I was convinced that the initials 'PC' upon the pouch were a coincidence, and not those of Peter Carey!"

"And how did you find him?"

"I spent some days in the East End, devised an Arctic expedition, put forth tempting terms for harpooners who would serve under Captain Basil – and behold the result!"

"You must obtain the release of young Neligan as soon as possible," said Holmes. "If you want me for Cairns' trial, my address and that of Watson will be somewhere in Norway – I'll send particulars later."